## "Willie, we should stop digging," Jake said abruptly.

She looked up at him. He rose to stand, holding Timber by his collar. Willie's gaze slid down to the spot he had dug. She could see all too clearly what the dog had found under the pile of debris.

"Is that...? Is that a human skull?" she asked.

"Yeah," Jake replied. "We need to leave everything alone—don't touch anything else. I'll call this in, get someone out here to gather the evidence so we can determine whose skull it is."

Willie felt numb and her hands dropped to her sides. The dirty leather bag slid off her lap, landing on the dusty ground. A tarnished key chain shaped like the letter K was still clasped to it. The world around her seemed to go fuzzy and she struggled to speak.

"I think I know whose it is..."

Slowly, she looked back up at Jake and met his questioning gaze.

"This is my mother's purse," she said.

Not the typical pastor's wife, **Susan Gee Heino** has been writing romance since the first day her husband bought her a computer, hoping she would help him with church bulletins. Instead, she started writing. A lifelong follower of Christ, Susan has two young adult children and lives in rural Ohio. She spends her days herding cats and feeding chickens, crafting stories with hope, humor and happily-ever-afters. She invites you to sign up for her newsletter at www.susangh.com.

### Books by Susan Gee Heino

### Love Inspired Cold Case

*Grave Secrets*

# TEXAS
# BETRAYAL

## SUSAN GEE HEINO

**LOVE INSPIRED**
INSPIRATIONAL ROMANCE

# LOVE INSPIRED®
## INSPIRATIONAL ROMANCE

Recycling programs
for this product may
not exist in your area.

ISBN-13: 978-1-335-42611-6

Texas Betrayal

Copyright © 2022 by Susan Gee Heino

For questions and comments about the quality of this book, please contact us at CustomerService@Harlequin.com.

Love Inspired
22 Adelaide St. West, 41st Floor
Toronto, Ontario M5H 4E3, Canada
www.LoveInspired.com

**Printed in U.S.A.**

Let us therefore come boldly
unto the throne of grace, that we may obtain mercy,
and find grace to help in time of need.
—*Hebrews* 4:16

This book is dedicated to my son.
Jake Heino, I'm so very proud
of the young man you have grown into.
We always knew God had big plans for you!
You are a true hero.

# Chapter One

Willie Henner brushed back her windblown curls and took a long, deep breath of dry Texas air. How many times in her childhood had she climbed on her old pony and come out here to play on this very ridge, the rolling landscape of her grandfather's ranch sprawling endlessly before her? Mama had always said, "God willing, this'll all be yours one day, Willemina."

Well, God wasn't willing, and Mama had been wrong.

Uncle Roy owned Juniper Ridge Ranch now and had for many years, ever since her grandfather died. Willie had just found out he was planning to sell the place, without even mentioning it first or giving her a chance to make an offer. Not that she had that kind of money, of course. If Uncle Roy would just work with her or wait for her to talk to the bank, though...

But he wouldn't. When she called him this morning, he said he couldn't afford to wait. He had an interested buyer, and he intended to sell *now*. Juniper Ridge would be out of her reach, gone like so many other things she loved.

Willie kicked at a stone by her feet. The dust blew

up into her face, and the stone tumbled a mere two feet away. Typical. When would she learn to stop being surprised by disappointment?

To find out about the ranch sale today of all days, though! Maybe Uncle Roy didn't remember, but Willie did. This was the date, twelve years ago, that she'd suffered her greatest disappointment. It was the reason she'd called Uncle Roy to let him know she was coming out to the ranch in the first place, to throw sticks with her dog and enjoy quiet time alone on the land she loved. It figured that now—just like twelve years ago—she'd be asked to leave her old home.

To prove the point, Willie was interrupted by the crunching of boots coming up behind her. She whirled around, wishing she hadn't let her German shepherd run so far ahead on the trail. Willie relaxed only slightly when she recognized the uniformed man stalking toward her.

"I got a call about some trespasser out here," the man said, pausing to prop his foot on a rock as he pushed back his hat to study her. "I should have guessed it was you."

"Sheriff Richards, how nice to see you," she said. He would know she didn't mean it.

Jake Richards was the youngest sheriff Laurel County had ever seen. Just four years older than Willie, he was barely in his thirties. And he wasn't fully sheriff, either. He was considered "acting sheriff," a title given when the previous sheriff had to retire due to health complications. There was an election coming up in a few months that would determine if Jake became the actual sheriff or not.

Willie doubted he had anything to worry about,

though. Everyone loved him. Why wouldn't they? He'd grown up here, played on the football team, scooped ice cream at the church suppers and could ride a horse like he was born on one. It didn't hurt that he was six feet tall with a smile that could charm rattlesnakes. And every female in the county.

Except Willie. Despite the man's chiseled features, cowboy swagger and shiny silver star, her opinion of him had changed over the years. Sure, maybe she'd had a schoolgirl crush at one time, but not anymore. Today she glared down on him from her perch on a flat boulder and hoped he could see the dislike in her eyes.

It didn't seem to bother him if he did.

"You know the rules, Willie. If you're going to come out here, you're supposed to contact your uncle and get his permission."

"He's calling me a *trespasser*? I talked to the man just this morning!"

"And he gave you permission?"

"Well…the conversation sort of ended before we got to that part. But he knew I was coming out here today."

"And I guess you know he's planning to meet with some real-estate buyers today. He can't have random people wandering around out here."

"I'm not random. This was my grandfather's ranch."

Jake did a terrible job of hiding a frustrated sigh. "I know, I know. I'm sorry you and your uncle don't get along. But come on, let's get you back to your truck."

She clenched her jaw and dug in her heels. "I don't need you to throw me off my own family's land."

"Then consider it a friendly escort."

"I don't need that, either," she grumbled. "And I can't

go until I find my dog. I brought Timber along, and he's run off somewhere."

"Fine. I'll help you look for him."

"No thanks. Don't you have some campaigning to do, Sheriff? Some babies to kiss or glad-hands to shake?"

She knew she'd hit a nerve when he cleared his throat before answering. "The election is a month away. There's plenty of time for me to do my job today."

"Doing your job for my uncle." She sighed. "Just how much *has* he donated to you?"

All right, maybe she'd gone too far now. Jake glared at her with his steel-gray eyes, and she noticed a slight tic at the corner of his lip. There wasn't any hint of that famous charming smile.

"Look, Willie, your uncle called, and I came out here. It's my job, no matter who puts in the call."

"I had someone bust up my mailbox last month. I don't recall you rushing out to take the report."

"As I recall, you live in town, don't you? That's police jurisdiction. In this instance, I just happened to be in the area when your uncle's call came in, so I'm the one who showed up. Now, will you quit picking a fight and tell me which direction your dog went?"

She knew it was a waste of her time to argue. Jake Richards always did his duty. He'd just been doing his duty twelve years ago when he was a young deputy, fresh on the job and eager to do the right thing. Willie had been a scared teenager, trying to take care of her half sisters and half brother after their mother disappeared. Jake was probably proud of himself when he helped Children's Services put the kids in foster care. He said it was the right thing to do.

Willie never agreed with him, and she never forgave

him. Up until that time she'd admired Jake, looked up to him with something like starry-eyed awe. He was the big brother of her best friend, Jessica; he was a local hero. But Willie made the mistake of sharing her struggles with Jessica, and she shared them with Jake. Jake informed the authorities. It was his duty, after all.

But letting that old bitterness take over today was just childish and self-defeating. Jake thought what he did twelve years ago was right, and she knew he was wrong. Neither of them were about to change their minds now. It was over and done. She didn't need to open the wounds—they were still far too tender.

"That way," she said, pointing. "Timber went down into the gully, sniffing after something."

Jake made a show of generously motioning for her to lead the way. She rolled her eyes—so he could see it, of course—and hopped off her perch. Their feet churned up dust as he followed her around a rocky bend, then down a rutted slope toward the shallow ravine carved by years and years of annual flash flooding. Today it was bone-dry.

She called for her dog, but there was no sign of him. Farther ahead, the ravine disappeared behind a rocky outcrop. Since she couldn't spot Timber anywhere in the open, it seemed likely he'd gone around those rocks.

She and Jake walked in awkward silence. Willie almost wished he would chastise her again for venturing onto her uncle's ranchland uninvited. But he was quiet, just as he'd been all those years ago, when he stood by and let her family be ripped apart. She kicked weathered stones out of her way as they rounded the rocky outcrop. Timber still wasn't anywhere to be found, but the dry creek bed wound its way toward a grouping of trees several hundred yards away. One huge, gnarled live oak rose up over a clump of weedy cedars.

"There—I think I saw something moving by those trees," Jake said finally.

Willie put her hand out to shield her eyes from the sun's glare. The trees seemed to spring from another outcropping of rock. The creek bed was rutted and deep.

"I don't see anything," she admitted.

Jake leaned in toward her, pointing so she could more easily follow his sight line. She shrank back from his nearness, partly because she was angry at him, and partly because she remembered being a fifteen-year-old girl with a hopeless crush.

"There, near those rocks," he said.

Now she could make out the black-and-tan figure of her dog. He was pawing at the ground, focused on whatever little creature he'd been after.

"Timber!" she called.

No response. The dog was clearly hot on the trail of something he wanted. Willie realized she'd have to get closer for her calls to catch his attention.

She jumped when Jake whistled loudly.

Timber glanced up. Before Jake could brag about his superior dog-calling skills, though, Timber made eye contact with them, then went right back to digging in the dirt. She had to laugh—Jake seemed so disappointed the dog would ignore him.

"I guess whatever he's found over there is much more interesting than either of us," he said.

"Yeah, he likes to think he's a brave hunter." Willie sighed. "Thanks for helping me find him, but we'll be okay now. You can go back to sheriffing. Just tell my uncle I'm not some dangerous cattle rustler or a poacher, okay? I'll get Timber and we'll head out."

But Jake didn't take the hint. "I'm here, so I might as well stick around."

"There's no need for you to stay."

"I think I will, just the same."

Now she was frustrated with him and let him see it. "Seriously, Jake? What horrible crime do you think I'm going to commit out here, trespassing on my own family's ranch? Or do you still just love dragging people from their homes?"

"That's pretty low, Willie. You keep vilifying me for doing the right thing over a dozen years ago?"

"It was wrong then and it's wrong now, Jake. You know it's true!"

"I know you were just a kid, Willie, that's what I know." He practically growled at her. "Your mother took off and left you with two grade-schoolers and a toddler. You couldn't take care of them on your own!"

"I was doing just fine!" she snapped back. "You saw for yourself—Abby and Mac didn't miss a day of school, little Maggie was clean and well-fed, the house was in order—"

"You were being evicted," he interjected. "Your electricity was turned off. How did you expect to pay the bills? Your mother abandoned you with nothing."

"She didn't abandon us!"

"Oh? Well, then where is she now, Willie?"

It was heartless for Jake to bring this up, to remind her of her failures. Maybe she shouldn't have goaded him, but this was just too much. He had no right to confront her this way, to remind her of the pain. And it was downright cruel to make her admit the truth.

She hissed the words at him. "She's gone, okay? She never came back."

"And Children's Services made sure you and your siblings got the care you needed," he said. "I know it was awful... I hated to be involved in it. But look where you are now. Everything turned out for the best."

No, it hadn't. She held back her argument, though. Jake couldn't understand; he had no idea what it was like to have his family torn apart, to literally lose his only parent, then watch his siblings shuffled off to various foster homes with a lifetime of belongings gathered up in old shopping bags. Sure, things had improved over time. Willie came to live here at the ranch for a while, she finished school and started a career, and her siblings seemed to be doing well, too. But everything had *not* turned out for the best.

The *best* would've been for someone to have found her mother and brought her back home, for Willie and her siblings to have been raised together under one roof, for her to have not had to grow up so soon. The *best* would've been for her to have had the life she'd expected—a loving mother, friends who didn't call Children's Services and a permanent home here, on Juniper Ridge.

"What does your dog have over there, anyway?" Jake asked, an obvious ploy to change the subject.

She was going to call him on his tactic, but it seemed to be legitimate. Timber really did have something, and he was digging at it, tugging determinedly. Whatever he'd been after, it looked as though he'd found it. Knowing the rugged landscape in this area, Willie realized there could be any number of native creatures hiding out in those rocks near the trees.

"That's all I need, for him to rouse up a skunk or a porcupine," she said.

"Come on then, I'll help you distract him."

Their argument was clearly over, and Willie turned her mind to her dog. Timber was still young and didn't have the good sense not to poke his head into a rattle-snake burrow or take on an angry javelina. With most of Willie's income going to put her brother and sister through college right now, she wasn't eager for a string of unexpected veterinary bills. She should've been paying closer attention and not let Timber wander off without her.

It would figure for Jake Richards to show up just when Willie had let something slip out of control. He must think of her as the most incompetent person in Laurel County. And maybe she was. She had failed her siblings all those years ago, after all.

The big dog had something in his mouth and was yanking it with all his might. Could he be pulling a snake out from under a rock? Willie rushed closer, calling his name.

Timber heard her this time and dropped his prize, wagging his tail in pride that he'd found something to present to her. Willie patted him in praise when she reached him, relieved to find that the thing he'd been tugging at was nothing more than some old trash wedged in with a pile of sticks under the rocks. It had probably washed up there during the rainy season a few months ago.

But what was it? Willie scratched Timber behind his

ears, holding him back as she crouched down to investigate. It appeared he'd found some kind of leather belt or a strap. Willie pulled at it.

The strap was connected to something that was still under the rocks, pinned there by the pile of debris. Timber was overjoyed she and Jake were taking an interest in his discovery, so he jumped about, going to another area of debris and digging intently. Clearly, he thought they'd come all the way down here to join in his game.

"At least it's not a skunk," Willie said, reaching to pull some sticks and clutter out of the way.

"No, but it looks like he's found something over here, too," Jake said, stooping beside Timber's new work area.

Willie focused on the leather strap. With one final tug, the branches and debris came loose. She sat back on her heels, still clutching the strap in her hands.

It turned out to be connected to a leather bag. A satchel? A handbag, perhaps? She extracted it and brushed it off. It took a moment for what she was seeing to register in her mind.

"Willie, we should stop digging," Jake said abruptly.

She looked up at him. He rose to stand, holding Timber by his collar. Willie's gaze slid down to the spot he had dug. She could see all too clearly what the dog had found under the pile of debris.

"Is that…? Is that a human skull?" she asked.

"Yeah," Jake replied. "We need to leave everything alone—don't touch anything else. I'll call this in, get someone out here to gather the evidence so we can determine whose skull it is."

Willie felt numb and her hands dropped to her sides. The dirty leather bag slid off her lap, landing on the dusty ground. A tarnished key chain shaped like the letter *K* was still clasped to it. The world around them seemed to go fuzzy and she struggled to speak.

"I think I know whose it is…"

Slowly, she looked back up at Jake and met his questioning gaze.

"This is my mother's purse," she said.

# Chapter Two

Jake tried to keep one eye on his investigators and one eye on Willie. She seemed awfully calm, standing under the sparse shade of a young sycamore tree. Her dog had plopped down by her feet, panting after his excursion. The first deputies on the scene were still questioning her about her find, and what she remembered about her mother's last days. It had to be a horrible experience for her, but she gave no indication of any emotion at all.

If she'd been anyone else, Jake would find her behavior suspicious. But this was Willie Henner. She'd made a life of hiding her emotions.

Everyone knew Willie's story. She lost her father when she was barely in kindergarten. Willie's grandfather had been happy to let his daughter-in-law and grandchild remain living on the ranch, but after just a couple years, her mother remarried and took Willie from her home here on the ranch to live cooped up in town. Willie's sister and brother were born there, but the home was not a particularly happy one. Willie's stepfather eventually abandoned the family, and her mother fell into a self-destructive lifestyle. At some point, Willie's baby sister came along, adding to her mother's struggles.

Willie's life had gone from bad to worse after that. Her grandfather became ill and passed away, then her mother disappeared…and finally the four siblings were separated. The image of Willie bravely comforting the terrified children as they were taken away was seared into Jake's psyche. Even then, Willie had worn an unreadable expression.

The only feeling she'd never been able to hide—and Jake saw it plain as day now, when she glanced over to catch him watching her—was the absolute contempt she felt for him. She hadn't tried to hide that, not ever. Jake had to admit, it was well deserved.

He'd known Willie since she was in grade school. Most older brothers would have probably ignored or been annoyed by their little sister's friends. Jake's little sister was special, though. She had a genetic disorder called neurofibromatosis, which caused skin discoloration, tumors inside her body and learning disabilities. She was also on the autism spectrum.

Jessica had trouble making friends. She was awkward and struggled in school. Most of her classmates recognized fairly quickly that Jess was not like them. Even when she tried, Jess never could keep up or fit in. Willie Henner, though, never seemed to care about that.

She and Jess shared a love for horses, the outdoors and art. How many times had Jake come home from football practice to find Willie and Jess sprawled on the screened porch with pages and pages of their drawings scattered everywhere with pencils, markers, crayons or paint? How many times had his mother sent him out to track her down when Jess was late for supper, knowing he would find his sister somewhere off with Willie? Too many to count.

But he'd ruined all that when he broke trust. Jess had confided in him, told him the struggles Willie had been having when her mother took off. It was Jess's heartfelt concern for her friend that tipped off Jake to what had been going on and eventually led him to notify Children's Services. Willie never forgave either of them. Jess had lost her best friend that day, and it was Jake's fault. The struggles she'd had after that, the painful turn her life had taken, still weighed heavily on him.

Now here was Willie, no one but a weary dog standing by her side while she endured yet another traumatic event. Twelve years ago, she'd been the only one who seemed certain her mother had not run away from her family. The rest of the town had been quick to label the woman a negligent mother. Regrettably, Jake had been one of them.

Based on items found near the remains, it seemed this was indeed Willie's mother. An investigation would have to prove it, of course, but from what Jake had seen, it appeared she'd been dead for those twelve years she'd been missing. What happened to her was a mystery that was going to be tough to solve after all this time.

Jake only hoped, for once, he might not let down Willie.

Noticing the older man picking his way over the rocky ground toward them, Jake smiled. At least Willie wouldn't be alone here anymore. The local justice of the peace, the man who would be handling the coroner's inquest for this case, had arrived on scene. Judge Torres was Willie's boss, her mentor and probably the closest thing she'd had to a father since hers passed away. Jake was very glad to see him.

"So we got us a mystery, Sheriff?" Judge Torres said, peering over the scene.

"We've identified the belongings—they were Willie's mother's things."

The man nodded. "So I heard. Sad, sad business... especially that she had to be the one to find them. How's she holding up?"

They were both watching Willie now, seeing her force a smile for the young deputy, who was carefully taking notes as he spoke with her. She glanced up and noticed Judge Torres. The smile became real at that point and she waved.

"I've got the scene secured, sir," Jake said. "My deputy seems to be finished gathering what he needs from Willie, so if you think it's all right, maybe we can let her go home now."

"I think that's a good idea. I'll stay behind and get the body ready for transport. Is it okay with you if I send her on to San Marcos? I don't think at this point a medical examiner will do us much good—we're going to need the forensic anthropology department."

"It's your call, Judge," Jake said. "And I think you're right. Is Willie going to be okay with that?"

The older man nodded. "Yeah. She knows how it works. We'll get her mother back here soon enough, then she can finally lay her to rest—if it really *is* her mother, of course."

Jake gave a sigh. "The purse still had her wallet with ID in it. Willie recognized a shoe we found down here, too. I think San Marcos will confirm this is Kim Henner Milson."

"I just hope they can shed some light on what happened. That poor girl sure deserves some answers after all this time."

"Yes, she does." Jake couldn't have agreed more.

Leaving the judge to his work, Jake shook the tension out of his shoulders and went to relieve his deputy from keeping an eye on Willie. The young deputy seemed glad to give up the task. Jake wished he didn't have to take it on. He wasn't even within ten feet of her before he felt Willie's cold, critical gaze.

"Miss Henner had a lot of good information about the items found here on site," the deputy said, indicating the notes he'd taken. "She recognizes the key chain attached to the purse—it was a gift Miss Henner recalls giving her."

Jake had seen the key chain, metal with some flakes remaining of what must have once been bright blue paint. It was shaped like the letter *K*—Willie's mother was named Kim. Also, the weathered purse still contained her wallet. It was fragile from years of being battered by floods and parched by the sun, but he'd managed to find an intact driver's license inside. It confirmed what they already knew.

"Thank you, Andrews," Jake said. "If you're done here, go see if there's anything more that Judge Torres needs."

"Yes, sir," the deputy said. He gave Willie his condolences, thanked her for her cooperation and left them.

After a moment of uncomfortable silence, Jake cleared his throat. Worry radiated off Willie like heat off an engine in July. Jake wished he could do something to help, so he offered what assistance he could.

"Judge Torres sends his thoughts," he said. "He's going to have the remains sent to San Marcos."

"Good, that's good. I'd better see if he needs me to do anything—"

"He's more worried about *you* needing anything."

"I'm fine."

"If you'd like, I can drive you home."

Unsurprisingly, she declined his offer. "No thanks. I've got my truck."

"I know, but you've had quite a shock today. It might be a good idea to let someone else get your truck home for you."

"Do I seem like I'm too hysterical to drive?"

"I didn't mean to imply that... I was just trying to be helpful. I thought you might be tired after all this."

She shook her head. "No, I'll be tired once I've answered all the messages that keep popping up on my phone, and once I've told my brother and sisters that we finally know where Mom is, and once I've seen my uncle and asked him why pieces of my mother are scattered all over his creek bed. Yeah, then I'll be tired."

"There's no reason to believe he knows anything about this."

Her contempt for Jake was visible again. "I should have expected you to defend him."

"I'm not defending him. I'll have plenty of questions for him, you can count on that. I'm just reminding you that he's innocent until proven guilty."

She rolled her eyes at that one. "I don't need a lesson in criminal law."

No, she didn't. She'd worked for Judge Torres since high school and had put herself through college, gaining a paralegal degree. She knew the law every bit as well as Jake did—probably even better. Still, things sometimes got fuzzy when family ties and old emotional wounds were involved.

"I simply think you could save yourself a lot of trouble if you let me drive you home now…before a dramatic confrontation with your uncle."

She rolled her eyes, but her sigh told him she agreed. "Fine. There's plenty of time for that dramatic confrontation with my uncle later. Right now, I'd probably better let my brother and sisters know what's going on before they hear it from someone else. Based on the texts I keep getting, word is spreading fast."

"It always does here in Laurel County," Jake agreed. "But are you sure you want to be alone now? Maybe I could call Pastor Jeff. He and his wife could—"

"I'm fine," she snapped. "I won't be alone. My brother and sister just got home from college last night. They're here for the festival."

"You don't have to go break the news to them on your own then. I'm sure this will be difficult for them to hear. I could go with you or send our chaplain over."

This time he detected a slight pause before she rejected his offer. Her anger seemed to be dissipating as exhaustion was setting in. "No. That's okay. To be honest, I really don't think they'll be too upset by it."

"Of course, they will. How old were they when she disappeared? It must have been hard for them to lose their mother at such young ages."

"Abby was ten and Mac was seven," Willie clarified. "And Maggie was two. None of them claim to have many memories of our mother. I doubt Maggie will even care that she's been located after all these years."

Jake was familiar with all of Willie's siblings. At

age nineteen, Willie had managed to get custody of Abby and Mac. She'd raised them through their teen years and now was putting them through college. From all accounts, she'd done a great job giving them all the stability and advantages she'd never had. Maybe Willie was correct in assuming they wouldn't be overly upset to learn what had been discovered here today. Given their mother's many struggles, Willie had always been more of a mother to them than a sister. Perhaps they hadn't felt Kim's loss as much as Willie had.

The youngest sister was a different story. Years ago, the court felt Maggie had bonded with her foster family. At her young age, it was decided she would do best to remain with them, so Willie wasn't granted custody of her baby sister. Instead, Maggie had been adopted and raised by the local couple, who were now her parents. Willie had been allowed to fill the role of auntie for the girl, but she'd not raised her as she had the other two.

Maggie was turning out to be quite her own person. However, Jake had encountered her on a professional level several times in the last few months. He wondered if he ought to give Willie a heads-up on the matter, since clearly she intended to contact her youngest sister today. But what could he tell her? He was bound by law not to divulge information on a juvenile.

And that's what Maggie was now, a headstrong four-teen-year-old who had made some questionable friends and some equally questionable decisions. Thankfully, she'd not gotten into any serious trouble. She'd been close, though. More than once she'd skipped school, been picked up at parties and was caught after curfew in a car with a much older boy, whose license had already been suspended. Her parents were determined to rein her in and had treated Maggie's rebellious behavior as a private matter. Jake wasn't sure how much Willie knew about any of it. He suspected very little. Finding out about it today, along with everything else, would certainly be quite a blow.

"I'd better get going," Willie said with a quick whistle for her dog.

Timber slapped the dirt with his tail and gleefully leaped up to accompany her.

"If you won't let me drive you, let me at least walk you back up to your truck," Jake said.

Willie simply shrugged. "I guess I can't stop you."

It was as close to an invitation as he would likely get, so he fell into step with the dog. Willie gave Judge Torres another wave and Jake called a few instructions to his deputies as they passed. Willie didn't slow down, and before long Jake was trailing her out of the dry creek bed and up the ravine. All the busy investigators were left behind. Their voices faded on the brush of the breeze.

It wouldn't be a long walk back to Willie's truck, especially at the pace she was keeping, but Jake was determined not to walk it all in silence. He'd been friends with Willie Henner once, and he felt it was time this feud between them stopped. More than ever, they needed to patch things up.

"I don't suppose you've heard that Jessica is back in town now," he said bluntly, for lack of any better way to introduce the topic.

"I've heard. Just in time for the Heritage Festival."

"It's always been her favorite time," he said. "She found a nice house to rent. Her daughter loves being just across from the park. She's seven years old already. You'd like her—she's quite an artist."

"That probably makes Jess happy."

"It does. She's doing really well, most days."

"That's good to hear."

He was hoping she might ask more questions, show some personal interest in his sister. She didn't.

"Jess would love to see you again," he said after a moment.

"It's a small town. We'll probably bump into each other at the grocery or the gas station at some point."

"I hope you do. Life has been pretty hard on Jess these last few years."

Willie paused, the dust settling around them as she turned to face Jake squarely.

"Look, I'm sorry for whatever she's been through, and I hope she and her little girl are in a good place now, but I just don't have anything to say to Jess. We're not kids playing on your back porch anymore."

"No, you're adults now. What happened when you were kids was a long time ago," he said, though he knew the last thing she needed was any additional reminder of the past. "Don't punish my sister after all this time for just trying to help her best friend. If you still need someone to blame, that's me. Jess was only a kid back then, just like you. At least I was an adult."

"Barely."

"I was old enough to know you needed help. Jess knew it, too. She cared about you, Willie."

"She should have cared enough to trust me to handle things."

Jake took a deep breath. They could go in circles like this all day, he supposed, and it wouldn't change Willie's mind. That was fine. It wasn't her mind that needed to change, it was her heart. His sister needed that more than ever.

"Just think about it, please," he said once he could trust his voice to remain calm. "Reach out to her. She could really use a friend, and after today... I'm going to guess you could, too."

"I'll be just fine," Willie insisted. "And so will Jess. She's got you, right? The perfect brother who always does the right thing for everyone."

"Willie, I—"

"You've got an investigation to run, and I've got to get home. My truck is just over that next ridge." She pointed ahead to the trail winding around another rocky outcropping. "Thanks for the escort this far, but I think I can find my way without any more trouble."

The words were barely out of her mouth when a man came into view, stirring up dust as he stomped toward them on the path. Willie took a backward step, clearly startled. She stumbled on a rock and nearly lost her footing. Jake was quick to catch her elbow and steady her, but all he got for his trouble was a frosty glare as she pulled her arm sharply away.

So much for his hopes of reconciliation. He took some small comfort in realizing that Willie's gruff attitude might actually not be entirely his fault. Her angry gaze quickly shifted from Jake and went back to the man approaching: her uncle.

Her animosity was lost on him, though. He stared right past her and pinned his focus on Jake. He didn't bother with casual greetings before launching into a string of heated questions.

"What is all this, Richards? Cruisers, trucks driving

over my land! What's going on here? Your office says someone found a body in my creek bed?"

"That's what's going on here," Jake confirmed.

"A *human* body? Are you sure about this, Jake? Maybe coyotes dragged a deer down there or something."

"It's *not* a deer. My investigators are going over the site now."

"Who found it?" the man demanded.

"I found her," Willie announced. "And hello, Uncle Roy. It's good to see you, too."

"*You* found her? What do you mean, found *her*? It's been identified already?"

"There were some items with the remains. They included identification."

Jake watched the other man's expression closely. Was this new information to him, or had he been aware of what they might discover down there? Roy Henner was a hard man to read. There was no immediate sign of recognition, no nervous furrow in his brow. From all he could see, Jake had no reason to think this was anything but a complete surprise to the rancher.

"So who is it?" Roy demanded.

Willie practically snarled at him. "It's my mother."

*The slightest hint of a tic.* It was almost undetectable, yet there it was. A glance at Willie told him she'd noticed, too. Uncle Roy was surprised by what she'd uncovered, but his reaction to the identity was something other than sheer astonishment. Whatever that fleeting moment of emotion had been, Jake couldn't be sure. All he knew was that Willie mentioned her mother and Roy reacted.

"Didn't you say you needed to get on home?" Jake

asked quickly, sensing Willie might dive into that dramatic scene Jake had been hoping to avoid.

She glared at him again but nodded. "I did say that.
I assume you'll keep me updated on everything?"

"Of course."

Thankfully, Willie merely called to her dog and refrained from whatever insult or accusation she may have
been considering for her uncle. She knew, like Jake did,
that he'd have a far easier time questioning Roy Henner
if the man were not seething with rage. Willie's impressive ability to contain her emotions was quite an asset in
this situation. She knew this was not the time or place
for confrontation, so she simply held it all back. Willie may have chided Jake for being the one who always
did the right thing, but the truth of it was that she held
that title completely.

Jake had seen that side of her all along, for as long
as he'd known her. His sister's limitations as a child
meant she couldn't do all the things Willie liked to do,
so Willie simply found things they both liked. In order
to get custody of her siblings, Willie didn't study art
after high school, as she'd always dreamed. Instead, she
worked a full-time job and studied something practical.

She might have snubbed Jake for all these years,
but he'd kept an eye on her. Willie always did the right
thing, no matter how much she had to sacrifice for it.
Walking away now was just one small example of Willie's iron will. Despite whatever anger she still harbored
toward Jake, whatever past grievances or current suspicion she might have for her uncle, she did the right
thing and let it slide.

After just discovering her missing mother's remains.
Jake tried not to be so in awe of her. He had to admit

defeat when she tossed her chestnut ponytail over her shoulder and produced a defiantly sunny smile.

"I'll see you later, Uncle Roy," she said, though her voice was brittle. "And you, too, Sheriff."

Then she ruffled her dog's ears and went jogging around the bend. In a moment, all that was left was a puff of dust from the path and the weight of an ongoing investigation. He stared after her longer than he should have.

"So where did she find these human remains?" Roy asked gruffly.

"On the other side of that ridge," Jake replied, coming back to the moment. "I'll take you down there."

He wouldn't let Roy actually enter the perimeter they'd set up, but the rancher might have some information to add. There might be another tic to observe, some telling behavior to indicate Roy knew more than he was letting on. Or maybe Roy had useful information. Maybe he remembered the name of someone Willie's mother had known all those years ago, someone who might have wanted to hurt her. Maybe Roy would turn out to be an asset to this investigation.

Jake almost laughed when he tried to imagine convincing Willie of that.

# *Chapter Three*

Willie watched Mac and Abby's expressions, breathless as she waited for their reactions. It was a lot to dump on them right now. They were both taking full class loads at the university and had just come home to enjoy the Heritage Festival for a few days. This news was bound to catch them off guard.

"You mean she's been dead all this time?" Mac finally blurted out.

"It looks that way," Willie said. "They'll have to finish the investigation, run some tests and things, before they can say for sure how long she's been…dead."

"But you recognized her things," Abby pointed out. "She disappeared twelve years ago, and you just found her with the things she had that very day. Obviously, she didn't just go on vacation for a while and then come back to die on your uncle's stupid ranch."

It was clear from Abby's tone she was distressed and angry. Mac, on the other hand, seemed uncomfortably calm.

"I'm actually glad she's been dead all this time," he said. "Yeah, I am, because that means you were right and everyone who told us she'd run off was wrong. It means we weren't abandoned."

Willie cringed at his bold words. Abby chastised him.

"That's kind of morbid, Mac. Maybe have a little sensitivity?"

Willie sensed the tension escalating, and that was the last thing she wanted. Of course, something like this would make emotions run high, but more than ever her siblings needed to stick together.

"It's okay, Abby. Mac is entitled to his feelings. We all are. This is a big deal, and it's going to take all of us a while to come to terms with it."

"But you've got to agree, it's better to know she's been dead all along than to keep wondering why she left us," Mac said.

"And wondering why she didn't come back, or at least contact us," Abby added.

"I'm glad you feel a sense of relief over this," she said calmly. "In a way, I do, too. I don't have to worry about Mom anymore. I know she's at peace and has been for a long time. But…"

"But?" Abby prompted.

"But the fact is that we still don't know what happened."

"We don't know *how* she died, or *why*," Abby said, finally getting to the heart of it.

"That's right," Willie nodded. "While Sheriff Richards is looking for those answers, people around here are going to be making some of their own assumptions. We might not like those very much."

"Assumptions?" Mac asked.

"Like when she first disappeared. Remember how

horrible that was? People started rumors that she was on drugs or she was just a bad person, that she didn't even care about us."

"I'd forgotten all that," Mac said. "Not sure how, though. I got in trouble at school for fighting with Trent McElroy over some of the awful stuff he said about her."

Willie tried to ignore her own memories as they bubbled up from the past, though she'd prayed every day to forget. The prayers hadn't worked, though. Probably because God wanted her to learn from the memories, not forget them.

"I'm sorry to have to put you guys through that all over," she said with a sigh.

"Don't be sorry! You aren't putting this on us," Abby declared. "This is going to be tough on all of us, but we're in it together. No matter what people in town say, no matter what crazy theories they start tossing around, I'm not going to let it get to me, and you shouldn't, either."

"She was our mom, too," Mac declared, "and we know she wasn't any of the bad things people said she was. I'm going to make sure the sheriff finds out what happened to her, even if I have to quit school and stay here."

"Oh, no," Willie said, quick to remove that option. "You will *not* quit school. Mom wanted all of us to get an education. You will both go back to school after the festival and finish out this semester. I'll be here. I'll keep an eye on the sheriff and make sure he's doing his job."

"But how long will that take?" Abby asked. "I mean… before we go back up to school, shouldn't we have a funeral or something? Can we do that before he's done investigating?"

Willie hadn't even begun to think about that. It hit Willie like a wave, a heavy wall of realization. *Her mother really was gone.* She was surprised to find that deep down inside, she had still been clinging to some tiny mote of hope that she might find her one day. Well, it was time to let go of that hope. She needed to think about how to find closure now, despite the ongoing investigation.

"It'll take some time," she said. "I don't know when we'll be able to do that."

Certainly, the burial would have to wait until the forensic anthropologists in San Marcos finished their work, but even that wouldn't go on forever. At some point, she would need to find an undertaker, make arrangements, coordinate with the church, with the cemetery, with her work schedule, with her siblings—all the things that should have happened years ago.

But hadn't she been praying for a way to bring her family closer together again? Maybe the timing of this discovery—during Heritage Weekend, when Abby and Mac were both home for a few days—was meant to be? God knew they'd need to lean on each other. Could this be part of the path to bring them all closer?

"What about Maggie?" Abby asked, interrupting Willie's thoughts. "Have you told her yet?"

Willie shook her head. "Not yet. I'd better call her parents."

It seemed such a strange thing to say, that she would call her sister's parents to tell them Maggie's mother died. As if she hadn't been dead to them all these years. Maggie claimed she had no memory of the woman at all, said she didn't even remember being a part of *this* family. She had only been a toddler, after all. At least Willie had been a few years older when she lost her father. She didn't have a lot of memories of him, but she did have a few. Maggie's new family was all she had known. How would she feel to learn their mother had been found?

"Are they still not letting you see Maggie?" Mac asked, accompanied by a dismissive smirk.

Willie was quick to correct him. "They've never prevented me from seeing her. The Westersons have always allowed us to remain part of Maggie's life. It's just lately…well, Maggie's life has been pretty busy."

"Too busy for us, that's for sure," Mac grumbled. "She didn't even bother to text back when I congratulated her for making the volleyball team."

"She made the volleyball team?"

It hurt Willie to realize she knew so little of Maggie's activities. Maggie and her adoptive parents lived ten minutes away, but the older Maggie got, the less Willie and her siblings got to see her. Mac seemed to want to blame it on her parents, but Willie knew it was more than that. Maggie had pulled away, not wanting to consider herself a part of their family anymore for some reason. How would she react now, with this sudden news? Would it make her push even further away?

"Don't worry about her, Willie," Abby said. "When we get around to planning a funeral, Maggie will either come to it or she won't."

"But she was Maggie's mother, too," Willie said, not able to shrug her off so easily. "Maybe when I talk to Mrs. Westerson, I can remind her that—"

Willie's phone rang, causing her to jump. Her nerves

were getting more frayed by the minute. A quick glance told her she needed to take this call.

"I'm sorry, I have to get this," she said. "It's my boss."

"Tell him we say hi," Abby said, ducking out of the room, apparently happy to abandon their conversation.

Mac was already in the kitchen with his head stuck in the fridge. The two of them certainly appeared to be taking today's events much better than she was.

"Hello, Judge," Willie said after a deep breath.

"Thanks for listening to good advice and heading home today," Judge Torres said. His deep voice contained fatherly compassion. "I'm so sorry for you, kiddo."

"Thanks. It was kind of a shock, that's for sure."

"I can only imagine. So Sheriff Richards was with you out there?"

"Yes, he'd come out to boot me off the land for trespassing when I...you know, when I found her."

"I'm glad you weren't alone. He's a good man, Willie. I know you've got your issues with him, but he'll see that the case is handled well."

"If he's not too busy trying to get re-elected."

"Now, Willie. Didn't you listen to Pastor on Sunday? If God can extend the fullness of His grace on us, we can certainly share a little bit of it for each other."

"Sorry, I wasn't there on Sunday."

"That's too bad," he said and she sensed he wasn't letting her off the hook. "The lesson was from Hebrews, a reminder that the Lord helps us obtain mercy to find grace to help in time of need. Sometimes this is about us and our time of need, and it's a wonderful promise that we will find grace. But sometimes it's about others and their time of need, Willie. If you haven't been approaching God for His grace, how will you have any of it to share?"

"Well, Uncle Roy certainly could use a little grace to share," she muttered. "I just hope he lets the sheriff do his job. We've gone too long without any answers."

"I pray that you'll get them. In the meanwhile, Willie, I want you to take as much time as you need. I'm sure your brother and sisters will need you, and you'll have arrangements to make. Don't worry about things at the office."

"But the festival starts up tomorrow! We've got the parade and then the carnival opens. I'll be there to make sure it's all running smoothly, sir."

"You've already done all the work," he assured her. "Don't push yourself now. If you need some time off—"

"I don't! I'd rather be working than just sitting around stewing over things."

She paused when she glanced up at the clock. Her heart clenched in panic. It was after noon already! She'd only planned to spend an hour out at the ranch, then be home in plenty of time to grab lunch and head in for a one-o'clock meeting.

"Oh, no!" she exclaimed into the phone. "The meeting with the fire marshal!"

"I've got this," Judge Torres assured her. "That's why I'm calling you. I've got your notes, you've already gone over everything. The contractor set up the big tent exactly as you specified, and the city has already signed off on it. The fire marshal just needs to do a quick walkthrough and make sure everything's in place, and it is. You do good work, Willie. Everything will be ready for opening ceremonies tomorrow."

"I need to double-check on the permits for the parade."

"I had Cindy take care of that when they called me out to the ranch and told me what happened. We're fine."

"And the caterers for the VIP dinner on Saturday? Have they called to confirm yet?"

"I got an email—their numbers match your numbers, so things look good there, too."

She was relieved to hear this. The last thing she could handle right now was some giant snafu for the festival. Of course, she didn't want to leave poor Judge Torres handling everything on his own. His workload was already heavy, considering how involved he was in so many aspects of the community.

"I should come in this afternoon," Willie said quickly.

"No, you should be with your family. How are your brother and sisters taking the news?"

"Abby and Mac seem to be handling it remarkably well," she admitted.

"And the little one?"

Willie took a slow breath before she answered. "I haven't told her yet."

"Then you've got no business coming into the office. Family comes first. Go over to Maggie's house and talk to her. I know you haven't seen much of her lately, so this is the perfect opportunity to reconnect."

It was true. Judge Torres was a wise man, and Willie had learned to take his advice. She'd been planning to call Maggie's parents, but a visit would be much better.

"You're right. I'll head over there once school lets out in a couple hours."

"School is out now," the judge reminded her. "They only had half a day."

It was a long-standing tradition in town to let school out early the day before the Heritage Festival so everyone could get ready for it. Local businesses, churches and civic organizations all decorated floats for the parade tomorrow. There were horse clubs and cultural dance groups and historical costumes. Many families used this event as a time to host reunions, with relatives traveling in from all over the country. Willie should have remembered there was no school this afternoon, tomorrow or Friday, either.

"I'll go over there right now," Willie said.

"Good. It'll be better if she hears about this from you first. I'll call if anything comes up, okay?"

He let her go after a few other words of encouragement. She was beyond blessed to have a boss like him; Judge Leland Torres was quite a man. Not only did he serve as a judge and justice of the peace, but he and his wife did volunteer work and chaired the Heritage Festival. He was always doing something to help their community.

He'd hired Willie to work in his law office when she was just an anxious teenager, fresh from her high-school paralegal certification program and desperate to be on her own. He needed much more than merely a paralegal, though. He needed an assistant who could help with all his various endeavors, and Willie was eager to learn. Once she'd proved herself capable, he helped her through the process of gaining custody of her brother and sister. Then he helped her get her college degree. Then he put her in charge of pretty much everything.

For ten years now, he'd been more of a father figure

than a boss. Judge Torres and his wife had helped her gain the life skills she'd needed to get by, to raise her siblings and to eventually complete her college education. She owed him everything, and it didn't feel right to pay him back now—when things were busiest—by abandoning her duties.

Come to think of it, Judge Torres would need her now more than ever. He was the Laurel County justice of the peace! In this part of Texas, that meant he handled the coroner's inquest for any suspicious deaths. Willie's discovery today certainly indicated a suspicious death. As his assistant, Willie would be helping him with the inquest, unless he decided that might be a conflict of interest. The law gave him the right to decide on that matter—she hoped he'd let her help.

The sheriff would be conducting a criminal investigation. He'd be searching for weapons, environmental factors, motives and suspects. The coroner's inquest would focus more on the body, the physical elements involved, the cause of death. Judge Torres would be the one to actually sign the death certificate. Given the state of the remains, he would likely be working with the forensics team in San Antonio.

None of it was going to be easy for Willie. She took a deep breath and tried to calm the frantic jumble in her mind. There'd be a lot to process, but for now she knew what she had to do.

Maggie came first. Word of their mother's discovery would be racing through social media. Rumors and theories would be rampant. Willie needed to get to her little sister and tell her what they knew, help her separate fact from speculation. Maggie deserved to know as much as the rest of the family did…even if it seemed she didn't consider herself part of it anymore.

During the ten-minute drive across town to the Westersons' home, Willie had to pull over at one point to let an ambulance pass. She was shocked when she turned onto Maggie's street and saw that same ambulance parked in her driveway! Willie's heart stopped cold.

The bright lights were flashing right in front of Maggie's house. A sheriff's cruiser was parked on the street, and people were milling around. Willie quickly parked her truck and dashed toward the house. What could possibly be going on?

She immediately ran into Sheriff Richards. He appeared in front of her on the sidewalk and called her name. She would have ignored him and run past if he hadn't grabbed her elbow and stopped her.

"Don't get in their way, Willie. Let them do their work," he said.

She tried to break free, but he held her fast. Angry and confused, she whirled on him.

"What happened? Why is the squad here? Where's Maggie? Is she all right?"

"She's fine, or she will be."

"She *will* be? What's wrong with her?"

"Slow down, Willie. Just stop. Listen to me!"

His voice was firm, but there was deep emotion behind it. That startled and worried her more than his forceful demands had. She stopped struggling against him and met his eyes.

"What's going on, Jake?"

"She's okay, I promise. Her parents just got here, so give them a few minutes."

"She was home alone?"

"School let out early today. Her parents were at work."

"So why is there an ambulance in her driveway?"

"Because she didn't come home alone," he said, then dropped his voice. "She wasn't supposed to have friends over, but she did. They got into some...trouble."

"What kind of trouble? What happened to her?"

"She's probably grounded, for one thing. Otherwise, she's fine."

"But the ambulance!"

"It's here for her friend. Look, I can't give out any details. They're kids, and kids do stupid stuff sometimes. One of her friends brought some alcohol."

Willie caught her breath. "They were drinking?"

"Her friend had too much, but Maggie did the right thing and called for the squad. As you can imagine, though, everyone is pretty shaken right now."

"Is her friend going to be all right?"

"I think so, but that's all I can tell you. Just trust that your little sister is going to be okay. At least, I'm sure she will be once Carl and Barb get done reading her the riot act again."

"*Again?* You mean...something like this has happened before?"

Jake winced and his gaze shifted. He obviously hadn't meant to give away so much. "You know I can't tell you that, either."

"How many times have you been called here to deal with this sort of thing, Jake?"

"It's not your business, Willie. You know I can't divulge anything like that."

"I can't believe it! We even talked about her today,

and you didn't think maybe you should mention my baby sister is some kind of juvenile delinquent?"

He hushed her, and she realized she was starting to sound a little bit unhinged. But how could she not? This day just got worse and worse. Her uncle was selling the ranch, the sheriff showed up to haul her in for trespassing and she'd literally stumbled across her own mother's remains! Why was she even surprised to find out that her baby sister was in trouble with the law after all this?

"You've had quite a lot of upheaval today," Jake pointed out. "Come on. Let's go someplace where you can decompress."

"No, I need to see Maggie."

"You're on edge, her parents are exasperated, and just between you and me, Maggie is in no frame of mind to hear about your mother right now."

Willie had to admit that made sense. There was no way she could approach Maggie in a calm, comforting manner in her current state. "Okay, you're right. But I need to tell her…"

"How about if I have one of my deputies handle the notification? It might be easier coming from someone who isn't…emotionally invested."

She drew a deep breath and sighed. She hated when he was right. "Fine. I guess I can come back later."

"Good. Now, how about taking care of *you*? Have you had lunch?"

"Um, I haven't really had time for that."

"Me, either. Come on. You can leave your truck parked on the street, and I'll give you a ride. How does Mama May's sound?"

She hadn't even thought about food, but no one could

say no to Mama May's Biscuit Barn. Her empty stomach growled at the very mention of it.

"Chicken and dumplings?" she asked.

He grinned at her. "The best in Texas."

"And maybe pie for dessert?"

"The sign out front said sweet-potato pie and lemon-meringue are the specials today."

"Not peanut-butter cream?"

"Mama May *always* has peanut-butter cream."

"Fine then. Let's go get lunch, but you're paying."

He just laughed at her. "Careful, I might start to think you don't hate me."

"You'll be glad to know that the way my day has gone, I'm too tired and hungry to hate anyone."

"Well then, not only will I enjoy my lunch, I might just enjoy the company, too."

Willie kept herself from smiling at his lighthearted jab. Despite everything, she realized she might enjoy lunch as well. And the company.

# Chapter Four

Jake had a hundred questions for Willie, but he knew better than to ask most of them. Today's discovery was a shock to her; it would rock their whole community. He'd face pressure to solve the case quickly, of course, and Willie was his best source for information. But now was not the time to grill her.

He could only imagine what she felt now; her world must be spinning. He needed to forget he was sheriff and just try to be Willie's friend. He wanted to support her in any way he could...if she'd only let him.

"I should let Pastor Jeff know what's going on," he said as they sipped coffee, waiting on their lunch orders. "His wife can add your family to the prayer chain, if you'd like."

She seemed startled by the suggestion. "What? Oh, no...that's okay."

"But you will give someone a call there, right? I know our church family would love to reach out to you and your siblings."

"*Our* church family? So we're family now?"

The sharpness in her voice cut him. Given their past

history, he should have used other words. Just because they attended the same church hardly gave him the right to assume any connection with her. To be honest, his church involvement had been rather limited since he'd taken on the job as sheriff. She'd be right to call him on that.

"I'm sorry," he said. "I just meant there are a lot of good people at church who care about you, Willie. If you need anything, I know they'll be there for you."

She shrugged. "I suppose so, though I haven't been to Bible class in so long I wouldn't be surprised if most of the members have forgotten all about me."

"Not possible," he insisted. "I haven't been there much since I took on this new job, but I'm still a member and I certainly haven't forgotten about you."

He tried to sound lighthearted, but Willie didn't seem impressed by the humor he'd hoped for. He should have known better than to make jokes at a time like this.

"So we're both delinquent," she muttered. "Great. We've got something in common other than just discovering what's left of my mother's body."

Conversation paused as the server brought their meals. Jake waited for Willie to continue, but she didn't. Obviously, he would have to be the one to initiate further conversation.

"Look, Willie, I thought you could use a break from that business, but maybe not. Are you ready to talk about it? Is that what you'd rather do?"

"You do have an investigation to conduct, right?"

"Absolutely. But it's been a hard day for you, so if you'd rather wait…"

"I think my mother has waited long enough, don't you? I appreciate the lunch, but I'm okay. I'd really, really like to get started on figuring out what happened to her. If there's anything I can remember from back then that might help, I'm all for talking about it."

"All right," he agreed. "What do you remember about the days leading up to your mother's disappearance?"

She thought for a moment and chewed her lip. "Nothing. I don't remember anything—we were just doing what we usually did. It was a week before the Heritage Festival that year. I remember because it was so hard explaining to Abby and Mac that we didn't have money to go. The days leading up to that? She didn't seem upset or preoccupied at all. At least not that I noticed. Maybe I just wasn't paying attention."

"You were a kid," he reminded her. "Tell me what a typical day was like for you back then."

"Well, my mother usually went in to work early, so I got the kids up and fed them before school."

"Your mother was working?"

She frowned, seemingly surprised he would ask. "Yes, she worked at the local print shop."

"She did? I don't remember that."

"She worked in the back, mostly putting together orders for some of the businesses in town. Why?"

"It's just that…well, wasn't there talk about how she was out of work, maybe depressed?"

Willie nodded. "All the rumors about how miserable she was. People also talked about how she was involved with this guy or that guy, all of them with bad reputations."

"So that wasn't true?"

"She had some boyfriends after my stepfather left, yeah, and it's true that the guy she was with when she got pregnant with Maggie wasn't exactly husband material, but she wasn't the way people said. She wasn't going to leave us to run off with some man, and she wasn't just sitting around at home being miserable while we all went hungry. Sure, things were hard, and I know she made some mistakes along the way. She did change jobs a few times and not always by her own choice. There were some difficult times between jobs. It's true that she wasn't happy every day, but she wasn't ready to give up. And she was a good mother!"

"You always said she wouldn't have just abandoned you."

"And it looks like I was right," Willie said, her anger boiling to the surface again. "If only people would have listened to me then, maybe…well, maybe whoever did this to her could have been caught. Maybe someone could have even got to her before it was too late!"

"Wasn't she gone for some time before you told anyone?" he asked.

"So now this is *my* fault?!"

"Of course not. I just… If you were so sure she hadn't run off why didn't you—"

"Because I knew what would happen! I knew people would think the worst of her. I knew we'd all be taken away. Looks like I was right about that, too."

So here they were, back to that same argument. Jake tried not to feel defeated. They'd been here for twelve years now, and this new discovery only seemed to solidify her refusal to forgive him for his part in the past. Losing her home and her family was her worst fear come true. He could hardly expect her to just get over it, despite the pain that he still carried for how her subsequent actions affected his own family.

"I'm sorry about everything that happened back

then," he said, resigned to their current situation. "I realize we're never going to be best friends, but I do hope we can work together. We have no choice, really. I plan to take an active part in this investigation, and I suppose the judge is going to allow you to assist in his inquest."

"You think he shouldn't?"

"If he trusts you to be objective, of course, he should. You're good at your job, Willie."

"Well...thanks."

"So for now, why don't we just put the past behind us and focus on today. Can we do that?"

She shrugged and pushed the food around on her plate. "I suppose. But you'll have to agree to follow the investigation wherever it leads—even if it takes you straight to my uncle's doorstep."

"You think he's got something to do with what happened?"

"We found her on his ranch, Jake. That means something."

"True, but until we know *what* it means, we can't go around accusing your uncle."

"You're going to *defend* him?"

"No, I'm going to investigate him, and anyone else who was connected to your mother back then. We can't start laying the blame on one person before we've got any evidence. If we do that, we might miss out on the truth. You do want the truth, don't you?"

"Of course. I just hope I can trust you to get to it."

Jake clenched his jaw and tried not to let her see his frustration. How was he supposed to reply to that? He shouldn't have to beg for her trust. He'd been doing this job to the best of his ability since the first day he put on a uniform, and he wasn't about to slack off now.

She had her reasons to mistrust him, though. It would take time to get past that. But how long did they have? So much time had already passed since her mother disappeared. Now that she'd been found, the clock was ticking even faster. Anyone with things to hide would be racing to make sure their secrets stayed hidden. Rumors and misinformation would be circulating again—Jake would have to work fast to sort through the evidence before the truth became even more deeply buried.

He needed Willie to tell him everything she knew. He needed her to trust him. What could he do to prove himself, to get past the years of hurt that stood between them? It seemed before he could solve this twelve-year-old mystery, he would have to atone for the pain he'd caused when he rescued Willie's family.

Maybe, just maybe, he could start by offering the smallest olive branch.

"You're worried I owe your uncle something because of his involvement in my election campaign, aren't you?"

"Yeah, to be honest, I am."

"And you're upset I couldn't give you any information about the trouble Maggie has been in."

The scathing look she shot him was almost painful. "She's my sister! I have a right to know about this."

He struggled to keep his voice calm, for both of them. "Maybe you do, but I don't have the right to tell you about it."

"So you see why I might be a little hesitant to trust you for the truth?"

"Here's what I can do." He propped his elbows on the

table and leaned in. "Until this investigation is done, I won't let your uncle donate a penny to my campaign or give his support in any way. Will that be acceptable?"

"Well, it's a start. I guess we'll see how that goes. But what about Maggie? She needs my help now, and I don't know what to do for her."

"I can't talk about Maggie, sorry. But... I know someone who can."

She eyed him with suspicion. At the same time, he knew she was eager to grasp anything hopeful. "Who is it?"

"Maggie's been taking art classes. She's made pretty good friends with the teacher. I'm sure you could get some useful insight there."

"An art teacher?"

"At the community center. They've been working on a big display for the festival. How about we finish our lunch, then I'll take you over there."

"So you think this teacher will talk to me about Maggie?"

He smiled, realizing he'd somehow come up with a plan that just might benefit all of them. "I do. Oh, look, here comes our pie. Eat up, then we'll head out."

He could tell Willie still wasn't quite trustful of him, but there was no way she could turn down Mama May's pie. It might put her in a better mood, too. He would need that once they got to the community center and she found out who Maggie's art teacher actually was.

That would be when he'd find out if this was such a good idea or not.

Willie tried not to feel so comfortable on the drive over to the community center. She'd been ravenously hungry, so lunch had really hit the spot. Jake's prom-ise to distance himself from her uncle had only added to her feeling of well-being. When he'd promised to introduce her to Maggie's art teacher, she almost felt grateful to him.

Clearly, she'd been overly affected by the pie—that was the only logical explanation for such warm, gen-erous feelings toward Jake. So far, he still hadn't done anything to prove he'd handle her mother's investiga-tion with complete fairness, but then again, he hadn't done anything to prove he wouldn't. For now, she would cooperate with him and try not to have a bad attitude.

That wouldn't be easy. She was anxious about the upcoming festival and all the responsibilities she had, she was worried about Maggie and, of course, she didn't know exactly what she felt about discovering her moth-er's remains. Admittedly, she was still a bit numb. Nat-urally her nerves were on edge.

She could only hope Jake really was steering her in the right direction with this art teacher. If she could just get some insight into Maggie's life these days, maybe she could find a way to connect with her. She'd been a complete failure at that so far, it seemed.

"Come on in," Jake said when he parked the car in the lot next to the Laurel County Community Center.

She followed him into the low, rambling building with big windows and crisp interiors. It was the well-earned result of cooperation between many local orga-nizations and some grassroots fundraising. Judge Torres had overseen the building committee, and Willie had helped out through the whole process. Everyone in Lau-rel County was proud of what their hard work had ac-complished. The community center had quickly become a real asset, providing ample space for meetings, a food pantry and all sorts of activities.

Willie found herself smiling to think that the work she'd done years ago had resulted in a place where her youngest sister could enjoy art classes and make some positive connections. For so many years art had been an escape for Willie. She was glad Maggie was finding it equally enriching.

Jake led her through the wide, welcoming lobby and down a corridor painted with sunny murals. "The art class meets here, in this room."

Willie knew it was unlikely Maggie would be here today, given what had happened earlier, but both the sound of laughter and the smell of fresh paint assured her class was in session. It reminded her of happier days—canvases on easels, clay pottery wheels, trays of watercolor paint and papier-mâché. Willie hadn't expected to feel such a rush of nostalgia just walking into the room.

Even more, she *truly* hadn't expected to find Jake's younger sister leading the class.

"Jessica is Maggie's art teacher?" Willie hissed at Jake.

"Um, yeah. I probably should have told you that part."

He didn't look the least bit remorseful. Willie felt her chest tighten. She and Jess hadn't spoken in years! Yet here she was, standing just ten feet away, wearing a paint-spattered smock and encouraging a little boy in an oversize T-shirt as he carefully painted white trim on the cardboard barn he was working on.

Before Willie could make a hasty retreat, Jess glanced up and noticed them. Her eyes caught on Jake first and she smiled. Then she saw Willie. Her smile turned into cold surprise. Her eyes narrowed as she glanced back at Jake.

"Hey, Jess, look who I ran into today," he said. If he was trying to sound relaxed and innocent, he failed miserably.

Jess was never one for acting. She greeted them with politeness, but nothing more. "Hi, Jake. Hello, Willie. It's been a while."

"Yeah, um…hello, Jess. Jake told me you'd come back to town. He didn't mention you were teaching art now, though."

"Three days a week, two classes a day," Jess replied in her no-nonsense way. "I like working with the kids. But…why are you here?"

"It's been an eventful day," Jake said. "Can we speak with you out in the hallway?"

Jess glanced around her classroom at the dozen or so busy children. They seemed to range in age from kindergarten through young teens. "We're finishing up our projects for the art display at the festival tomorrow. Let me make sure everyone is okay, then I can step out for a couple minutes."

Jake agreed, and he motioned for Willie to follow him to the doorway. The room buzzed with creativity as they waited there. Willie smiled, watching the young artists as they worked.

"That girl over there, the one working with clay," Jake said softly, pointing to a studious little girl with red ringlets. "She's Jess's daughter."

Willie nodded. "Shaye? Yes, I see the resemblance."

"Except for that red hair." Jake chuckled. "She's the first redhead in the family."

"She must get that from her father," Willie said without thinking.

The mention of Jess's ex-husband brought a quick reaction from Jake. "We don't talk about him."

"Sorry. I forgot things ended badly there."

"No, things *started* badly and just got worse. When Jess finally broke away from that man...well, that's when life actually got better for her and Shaye."

"That sounds awful. At least they're okay now, and Shaye looks like she's doing great."

"She is. Jess is a great mom. Now that they're back here, I'm not quite so worried about them anymore."

Willie would have liked to hear the story behind all that, but it was none of her business. She knew just from hearing people talk that Jess had gone off with a man who was older, and her marriage had been rocky. Willie should be relieved for her former friend.

Jess returned to join them and the adults stepped out into the hall, out of earshot from the kids, but where Jess could still look in and keep an eye on things.

It was good to see her again. Willie hoped Jesse felt the same, despite everything that had happened.

"Jake pointed out your daughter," Willie said softly. "She's beautiful."

"Thanks," Jess replied with a cool smile. "She's amazing. But what's going on? I don't usually get unexpected visitors."

"We thought you should know," Jake began, "that we made a discovery today. Willie's mom... Her remains were found."

The surprise was evident on Jess's face. It was not her nature to display emotion very often, so Willie knew the information had truly affected her. Obviously, she hadn't heard any rumors yet. There was no sentiment in her voice, no socially expected condolences or anything like that, when Jess simply asked, "Where?"

## Chapter Five

Willie realized she shouldn't have been surprised by Jess's cool reaction. Jess had always been like that— she spoke whatever was on her mind, without emotion. The fact that she was so straightforward was something Willie had once appreciated about their friendship. In a childhood so full of volatility and uncertainty, Jess had been solid and consistent. She was unfailingly honest, to the point of being brash at times. But Willie didn't mind. Jess was just… Jess.

The other kids might have called Jess weird or pushy or even unfriendly, but Willie loved the way Jess never created useless drama. She didn't demand attention for herself and didn't take the bait when others demanded it. Willie and Jess could sit peacefully together and just draw or go riding on the ranch in complete silence. Their youthful friendship had been the one place where Willie didn't have to be the moderator or the responsible one.

Feeling the chasm between them now brought a pang of regret.

Not that Jess seemed to feel it. She simply shifted

her expectant gaze from Willie to Jake. She'd asked a question and was just waiting for an answer. Willie cleared her throat.

"It was out at the ranch…in a dry creek bed at Juniper Ridge."

Jess took that in and nodded. "Oh. Okay. Good."

Now Jake seemed surprised. "Good? You don't mean that, Jess."

Jess looked confused that he would scold her. "She's been missing a long time. It's good that someone finally found her. Who was it?"

"I found her," Willie replied. "I was walking out there with my dog."

"She's been out there all along?"

"It looks that way."

"What happened to her?" Jess asked.

Jake cut in before Willie could answer. "We don't know yet, and we can't really talk about it."

Jess nodded. "Ah, ongoing investigation."

"Right," Jake agreed. "The sheriff's office is investigating, and there will be a coroner's inquest, too."

Jess seemed to understand, but she turned to Willie for clarification. "I see. Don't you do legal stuff like that with Judge Torres?"

"Yes, I'm his paralegal. He's in charge of the inquest."

She half expected Jess to raise some concerns. Jess liked to follow rules, so perhaps she was worried that there was a conflict of interest if Willie involved herself in the investigation, even if she was just assisting. But Jess said nothing more about it and, in fact, seemed to shrug off the whole thing.

"Well, I'm sure after all this time there isn't much

to investigate. I'm glad you've got some closure, Willie. Thanks for letting me know, but I need to get back to my class."

"No problem…" Willie said, too confused by Jess's dismissal to remember the real reason they came here.

But Jake hadn't forgotten. "Wait, Jess. There's something else. Something happened to Maggie."

Jess obviously had no idea whom he was talking about. "Maggie?"

"One of your students," Willie said. "Maggie Westerson. She's my sister."

Again, Jess showed little emotion. "Oh, right. What happened to her? Her mother texted to say she wouldn't be here for class today."

"She got in trouble, doing things she's not allowed to," Willie said. "I'm worried about her falling in with the wrong crowd, making bad choices, all that. Jake says maybe I should talk to you about it."

Now Jess did show emotion. She was angry. "So Jake told you I knew all about that sort of thing, hanging out with bad influences, making bad decisions, ruining my life and—"

"No, I didn't tell her anything like that," Jake interrupted. "I told her you'd kind of taken Maggie under your wing, befriended her. She should talk to you about Maggie."

Willie jumped in before any more hurt feelings could derail the conversation. "I was hoping you might have some insight, Jess. I've tried reaching out to Maggie, but I can't seem to get through. Jake thought that since she's taken to you so well, maybe you could share some pointers. How can I get her to trust me a little more?"

Jess gave Jake a skeptical glare, but her reply to Willie was cordial. "Maggie's a good kid. She's just at that age where she's trying to figure out where she fits in, that's all. Maybe it's been hard on her, going from one family to another."

"The Westersons were the only foster family she went to after they took her away," Willie said, trying not to let accusation creep into her voice. "Maggie stayed with them until the court granted them the right to legally adopt her. She claims she doesn't even remember being in any other family."

"And yet you're still there, reminding her all the time," Jess said.

"Of course, I remind her! I'm her sister."

"A sister from a family she can't remember," Jess said bluntly. "You've got to see how that might be hard for her, especially at this age. Is she a Westerson, or is she something she doesn't even know?"

"She's my *sister*," Willie repeated firmly.

"She's barely a teenager, and she's just your *half* sister. She's just a half sister to Abby and Mac, too, and she's not biologically connected to her parents at all! That must be confusing. She doesn't know who she is."

"If she'd ever return my calls, maybe I could tell her who she is," Willie grumbled.

Jess laughed out loud, though Willie hadn't meant it to be funny. "You can't tell her who she is! She has to find out for herself."

"Well, she's looking in all the wrong places," Willie said sharply. "Staying out late, hanging out with kids who drink, ignoring the rules. That's why I'm trying to help her."

"She's not looking in *all* the wrong places," Jess corrected. "She's been coming to art class, and she's really talented. I think it's great for Maggie to discover this part of herself. She's very creative."

"So that's why she's opened up to you." Willie sighed. "You connect with her through art."

It was hard not to feel a twinge of guilt at this realization. Maggie had inherited the same creative streak Willie had, yet somehow Willie never realized it. Art had been such a huge part of her own youth, but she'd gotten away from it with the responsibilities of life and adulthood. Maybe if she hadn't walked so far away from that part of herself, she would've been the one to unlock it in Maggie. Maybe she would have made the connection Jess had. Maybe she could have protected Maggie from the mistakes she was making.

"Isn't that good news?" Jess asked. "You're an artist—you and Maggie have that in common."

"Yeah. We do," Willie admitted.

Jess smiled in satisfaction. "Well, glad I could help. I really do need to get back to my class now. We've got a lot to get done for the show tomorrow. It's going to be great!"

Jake gave her a nod. "Those kids are doing some amazing work. You're an excellent teacher, Jess."

"Thanks." She turned to go back into the room but paused in the doorway to glance back. "Willie, I'm glad you finally know where your mom is. I guess knowing where her remains were found is going to make it a little easier to discover what happened to her."

Willie didn't quite see the logic in that. Jess must have seen the confusion on her face.

"You know," she continued. "You found her on your uncle's ranch. Of course, you can't discuss it, but it's pretty obvious that if you found her there, your uncle must have had something to do with putting her there. At least you know who your prime suspect is."

As if she'd said something as simple as "have a nice day," Jess strolled back into her classroom to ooh and aah over her students and encourage their efforts. Willie was left to glance up at Jake, and she wondered what he thought of his sister's parting words.

"She definitely speaks her mind," he said after a moment.

"Yeah. That's her best quality."

"And her worst," he added. "She just assumes foul play was involved."

"Well, don't we?"

He sighed. "Yes, we do. But you and I are professionals, Willie. There is no such thing as a 'prime suspect' until we have something more than just assumptions, right?"

"Of course," Willie agreed. "But you are going to question my uncle, right?"

"I told you I would."

"Great. There's no time like the present. Shall we be off?"

"Slow down," he said, overdramatically waving his hands. "I said I'd question him, but we've got to do things in order. First, I need a little more information before I just go barging over there asking what he knows."

"If you ask him what he knows, then you'll have a little more information!"

"Will I? You think if he knows anything that he'll just come right out and tell me?"

"No. I don't think he will."

"Then obviously I need to do a little more investigating first. Why are you so set against him, anyway?"

She didn't answer Jake right away. How could she explain years of grievances in just one brief conversation? She couldn't. Uncle Roy had seemed resentful toward her for as long as she could remember. Maybe it was because she'd been so close to her grandfather, and he'd had a more tenuous relationship with him. Maybe it was because Willie always felt so connected to the ranch, and Uncle Roy never could quite seem to find his place there.

Or maybe it was because Grandpa had expected Roy to look after his brother's family once Grandpa was gone. He clearly resented that, begrudging the money that had been left to her and treating her like an unwelcome guest in his home when he'd been more or less forced to take her in. Indeed, she had plenty of reasons to dislike her uncle. But none of them would matter to Jake.

"My uncle thinks I was a drain on him financially. He thinks I inherited too much, and he thinks I'm constantly expecting handouts. He'll make you believe I'm just a greedy whiner if I complain about him, because you're buddies and he's helping your campaign."

"No, Willie," Jake said, his voice surprisingly full of compassion. "I consider him a friend, but you're the hardest working person I've ever met, and you take life's punches and roll with them. I don't care what your uncle might say—there's no way I would ever believe you're a greedy whiner or looking for a handout."

"Really?"

"Really. And you think I would put campaign funding above learning the truth? Well, then you don't really know me. I *will* ask your uncle the hard questions, but I need to know what they are first. If you have some credible reason to think he might not have acted in good faith, I want to hear it. That's exactly the kind of information I need."

She was strangely encouraged by Jake's reaction. "Okay, fine. If you want to know the kind of person my uncle is—and if you'll believe me—I'll tell you."

"I want to know what kind of person your mother was, too. You can tell me all about both of them, and anyone else involved in your lives back then, over in my office."

"Your office? So now you're questioning *me*? Maybe I'm your prime suspect, then."

He looked her square in the eye. "No. You're my prime witness, Willie. I get that you aren't thrilled about having to work with me, but if you want to know what happened to your mom, that's how it's going to be. You're going to have to trust me, and I'm going to ask you to dig back into memories you might not want to revisit."

She wasn't proud of herself for snapping at him. He'd been nothing but kind to her today. Why would she lash out at him like that? It seemed everything about today was going off the rails, and she just didn't know what to do about it. What a disappointment she was—to herself and probably to everyone around her.

"I'm sorry, Jake. This whole thing is just…my nerves are on edge. I told the deputies what I knew twelve years ago, but okay. Let's go to your office and we can go over it all again."

"Thanks, Willie. I know this is hard. If you'd rather wait until tomorrow…"

"No, let's do it now. As you said, I'm your prime witness. From all the accounts when my mother disappeared, I was the last person to ever see her."

"Well, the last person to see her *alive*," Jake added.

Willie winced as an icy shiver crawled down her spine. Neither of them had come right out and said it, but Willie knew what he meant. Most victims of violent crime knew their attacker. If so, then Willie probably knew her mother's murderer, too. Maybe she still did.

## Chapter Six

Jake nodded at one of the dispatchers as he left the break room and headed back into the hallway. He'd gone in there to get coffee for himself and Willie. She was sitting uncomfortably back in his office, probably trying not to think about the last time she was brought here, to talk about her mother's disappearance. Even with the jumble her emotions must be, here she was, ready to let him ask her even more questions. True, some of the things she'd said to him today had stung, but he wouldn't hold them against her. Not after all she'd been through.

"Here you go," he said, startling her as he entered the room.

"Thanks."

She took the cup he offered and shifted nervously in her chair. He went around his desk and took a seat. His list of questions for Willie was pretty long. He'd only had a short time to pull out some of the files on this case, so he was basically starting from scratch.

With a deep breath, he offered a prayer for guidance.

The last thing he wanted was to bluster into this and cause Willie any more grief.

She'd lived with her mother's disappearance for so long, probably rehashed those last days with her over and over. He prayed to find the right words, the best questions to ask in the most sensitive way. The things he needed to ask her had no doubt been covered twelve years ago. It would be interesting to see what she said today, then compare that to her responses from the past.

Not that he expected her to lie to him. No, she'd never do that. She simply might have a different understanding of things now than she did at age sixteen. Her memories may have faded, but they also might have matured over the years, just as she had.

"All right," he began. "So you said that in those last few days before your mom went missing you don't recall anything out of the ordinary. Did she ever say anything that made you think she was worried? Afraid of anyone?"

Willie winced at his questions, but she took a deep breath and calmly replied, "No. I don't recall anything like that. Things were just…normal."

"And what was normal for you then? Your mom went to work and you helped with the kids?"

"She worked at the print shop, as I told you. Her boss was kind of a jerk."

"In what way?"

"You know, just making her life difficult because he knew she needed the job and she wasn't going to quit. Maybe that's why people said she was going to lose her job, because he treated her so badly. But he wasn't going to fire her—he needed her there. He gave her the work no one else wanted, like the rush jobs, the after-hours jobs, jobs for the extra picky customers. When she started working there, they agreed she wouldn't have to come in until after she got us all off to school or day care in the morning. Once she was working, though, her boss told her he needed her early, to get things ready for the day or whatever. So she had to start going in at six thirty, and I took over getting everyone where they needed to be for the day."

"The print shop has new owners now. Who was her boss then? Do you remember his name?"

Willie thought for a moment. "Um, Larry Pennel. I don't even know if he's still around. All I remember about him is his voice—his loud, angry voice. We still had an old answering machine then. When he couldn't reach Mom's cell phone, he called that and left messages. He was yelling, saying if Mom didn't show up for work she was fired."

"Yelling? He often left angry messages for her?"

"No, just after she disappeared. He left three messages that first day, and another one the next Monday."

"And you hadn't told anyone at that point that your mother was missing?"

"All I knew was she hadn't come home at night, and she wasn't there in the morning. I figured she'd be back any minute."

"Walk me through the police report. It says the day she disappeared started out normal. She went to work, you and the two older kids went to school and the little one went to day care, right?"

"Yes. I got the kids up, fed them, got them dressed, put Maggie in her stroller and walked everyone where they needed to be. We were living in town, on Magnolia Street. I dropped Maggie at the sitter's house, just a couple blocks over, took Abby and Mac to their school, then I went on to the high school."

He was taking notes, trying to get a mental picture of what Willie's life was like during that time. It couldn't have been easy, taking on that much responsibility at such a young age, but she'd done it. She'd done it so well, no one even realized how bad things had gotten for them by the time Jake found out their mother was gone.

"And you picked everyone up after school?" he asked.

She shook her head. "No, I had to go to my job that day. I worked at the grocery store three days a week, after school on Thursday and Friday, then half a day on Saturday."

"And this happened on a Thursday?"

"Yes. When I got out of school I went straight to my job, and Abby and Mac always went to the babysitter those days. When Mom got off work, she'd pick all three of them up and take them home. They'd have dinner, do homework, then Mom would drive over to pick me up when the store closed at eight o'clock."

"Who watched the kids then?"

"Abby was ten. Mom left her in charge for the half hour it took to get me."

"I see. So your mom picked you up as planned on Thursday night?"

"She did."

"And she seemed…normal?"

"I don't know. At the time nothing stuck out to me, but I've thought about it and thought about it all these years. Of course, there must have been something, but I just didn't see it."

"Then sometime in the night she left, and you never saw her again?"

"No, I know exactly what time she left. It was eight twenty-five that night."

He flipped through the pile of files on his desk. He remembered reading a few details about this case, but not the actual time of her mother's disappearance. That seemed oddly specific.

"How are you so sure of that time?" he asked.

"I noticed the clock in the dashboard of the car," Willie replied. "We pulled into our driveway, and Mom told me to go ahead inside and make sure the kids got their baths and made it to bed by nine o'clock."

"Wait…she just left you there?"

"She said she remembered something she had to take care of, but it wouldn't take too long."

This was news to Jake, and it seemed like fairly pertinent information. "Did she tell you where she was going?"

"No, just that she'd be back in an hour."

"An hour. Hmm…what else did she say? Was she meeting someone? Did she seem anxious or anything?"

"That's all I can remember, Jake. She said there was something she had to take care of."

"Those were her exact words?"

"Yes… I don't know. I'm sorry, Jake, but don't you think I've played that night over and over in my mind all these years? Don't you think I've questioned myself, prayed to God to remember more? But it's just…that's all there is. I was tired from a long day, I was grumpy that I had to take care of my sisters and brother, I was upset Mom didn't have time to go over the college application papers I brought home that day. I'd been eager to go over them with her. I think I babbled on about them the whole drive home."

"College application papers?"

She gave a sad laugh. "As if we had the money for me to go to college. But I was hoping for scholarships and financial aid."

"You wanted to study art."

"Mom always encouraged that, even though it wasn't really practical. But she knew how much I loved it and she wanted me to be happy. She said she'd help me fill out those applications."

"So when she remembered whatever it was she had to go do, you were upset about putting that off. She wasn't upset, but you were."

"I always regretted that. My last words to her were kind of snippy."

"What did you say?"

Clearly Willie would have much rather forgotten this part of the story. She stared down, clenching her hands in her lap. Jake could tell it cost her dearly to think back on those last moments with her mother.

"I told her it wasn't fair that I had to take care of everything. I told her I deserved to be her priority just once, that maybe her thing could wait tonight and my college applications could come first."

"What did she say to that?"

Willie blinked, cocking her head slightly. "I—I haven't even thought about that part of the conversation for so long. All I hear is my whiny teenage voice in my head, complaining about not getting enough of her attention. I think she said…she said not to worry, that she'd sort it all out and I would be able to go to whatever college I wanted."

"She was very proud of you."

"I should have thanked her, or hugged her, or told her I loved her or something. Instead, I just grumbled about her never having time for me, and I got out of the car."

It was difficult to see the raw emotion she felt. He'd never known Willie to let anyone see into her pain. He wished there was something he could do now to comfort her.

"You can't beat yourself up, Willie. You had no idea something would happen."

"What if maybe she *did* give me some kind of clue about where she was going, but I was too caught up in my own worries to notice? I'm sorry, I just don't know anything more."

"And I'm sorry I have to dredge this all up again for you. Are you okay to go on, or do you need a break?"

"I'm fine. What else do you need to know?"

Jake checked over his notes. He needed to know everything she knew, but he wished the cost wasn't so high. "I'm getting the timeline straight. The last time you saw her was eight twenty-five on that Thursday night. She left you at your house, and she drove off."

"Right. I told the sheriff then that I watched her car. She drove up to Main Street and turned right, going north. I assumed she was going to the print shop, since it was that way."

"But she didn't go there?" he asked.

"Not according to her boss when the police finally talked to him. He was out of town visiting family that day—that's why he was so mad when Mom didn't show up for work. He had to come back from his vacation."

"What time was it when you realized she should have been home?"

"I got the kids ready for bed and did my own home-work, so it was after ten o'clock before I realized how late it was. I tried calling her, but no answer. I tried the print shop, too, but it just went to voice mail. I was worried, but…well, when she was dating someone, she stayed out late sometimes, so it wasn't completely un-usual."

"Who was she dating at the time?"

She rolled her eyes at that question. "I don't know. Maggie's father had taken off before Maggie was even born, then there'd been some guy named Rob for a while, but when law enforcement questioned him, he said they split up and he'd been living in Houston, I think. I guess he had some sort of proof he wasn't around when she went missing. There was another man they said she had been seen with, but I didn't know who he was. His name is probably in those files somewhere."

"And the rumors about her being involved in drugs?"

"Just rumors! Yes, she had some trouble with that years ago, when she was with my stepdad, but after he left, she got better. Mostly."

"Mostly?"

"When she was with Maggie's dad…things were pretty bad for a year or so then, too, but when she found out she was pregnant with Maggie, Mom got totally clean and stayed that way."

"As far as you knew."

He could see her gear up for a fight, but she deflated almost immediately. "You're right, as far as I knew. It's obvious I didn't know what she was doing…not really. I guess she could have gotten in with the wrong people again. I just… I don't know."

"And that's why you didn't contact anyone when she disappeared."

"I knew her history with men and what people would think. And I honestly thought she'd turn up, that she'd have some logical excuse and everything would be normal again."

"But it wasn't. Why didn't her boss think to contact anyone when she was missing?"

"Because I called him," she said. "It was Friday when he left those angry messages. When Monday came and we still hadn't heard anything from her, I didn't know what to do. I was scared, but I didn't want my sisters and brother to be scared, too, so I tried to keep everything routine for them. I got them off to school and the sitter, then I went to school, just like any other day. I didn't have to work on Monday, so I picked them up after school and we all came home. There was another angry message from her boss, so I knew he didn't know where she was, either."

"So you called him?"

"I did. I made up some story about a sick relative that Mom had to go take care of. I said she'd be on leave until further notice and that if he wanted to fire her for it, that was okay. He just needed to send her last paycheck."

"He didn't even question why her teenage daughter was making phone calls for her?"

Now she gave him a weak smile. "I guess I'm a really good liar."

He laughed. "I'll keep that in mind."

"I think he just didn't care. Once the missing-person investigation started, the police decided he wasn't involved, and that was that for Larry Pennel."

"So Larry the boss was cleared, Ron the old boyfriend was cleared, but there might have been some other boyfriend you don't remember."

Jake started shuffling through the files again. The initial investigation had been started by the local police department since, at the time, Willie's mother had resided within the village limits. Due to manpower shortage, though, the police had quickly asked for help from the sheriff's office, so the information was filed here. It was clear nothing had been done since the case had been shelved years ago, when no further leads were discovered.

One file in particular caught Jake's eye—interviews with persons of interest. He flipped it open and started scanning. Willie leaned over to get a view.

"There...what does that say?" she asked, pointing to a note scrawled by hand in a margin.

The handwriting was sloppy, but Jake could make it out. He suspected Willie could, too. He wished he hadn't let her see it.

"It says 'possible connection to known offender,'" he said.

"What does that mean?"

He sighed. "It could mean anything. Someone just put this note there to flag the need for follow-up."

"Did they follow up? What's that little notation under it?"

"It looks like a case file."

"What case is it?"

"I don't know," he acknowledged. "But we can find out."

Sliding his chair to reach his keyboard, he quickly typed in the noted case-file number. Information began popping up. Right away he knew Willie wasn't going to like it.

She couldn't see his computer screen from across the desk. When he didn't supply details quickly enough, she hounded him. "What does it say? What sort of case is it?"

"Drugs," he replied, wishing he didn't have to. "It's a drug case."

She was visibly stunned. "And my mother is connected to someone involved in it?"

He scanned through, looking for names that stuck out. He didn't see Willie's mother's name, but his eyes stopped on one he knew. He knew it well—too well.

"What is it?" she said, clearly seeing something in his expression that concerned her. "Is my mother listed in that case?"

"No…it's someone else," he said, then on a whim went back to the paper files on his desk.

Someone had provided a listing of names of those who had been in contact with Willie's mom before her disappearance. There was the boss, the boyfriend named Ron, the family members…and one other name. This must have been that other possible boyfriend Willie mentioned, the man investigators had asked her about.

Well, maybe Willie didn't know the guy, but Jake certainly did. And according to this file, Willie's mother did, too.

"Who is it?" Willie asked.

He met her gaze. "Mason Bannet."

At first Willie's expression didn't change; she didn't know the name. Then it slowly sank in and he watched her brow wrinkle in recognition.

"Wait…" she said. "Isn't Mason Bannet the guy who…?"

"Ran off with Jess and treated her like garbage?" he said, finishing for her. "Yeah. That's who Mason Bannet is. My ex-brother-in-law."

## Chapter Seven

Willie wasn't sure she had heard him correctly. "Did you just say that Jess's ex-husband used to go out with my mom?"

He seemed as stunned by the news as she was. He scrolled through the computer and then turned to scan the pages on his desk. She couldn't think of anything else to say, so she just sat and waited for him to give her any kind of explanation.

"His name is right here," he said, finally picking up one of the files and showing her. "See? He was interviewed about your mother. The detective notes that her coworkers at the time identified him as someone who often met her after work."

"You mean…he was that mysterious other boyfriend?"

He scanned a bit more. "I don't know. But when they interviewed someone named Karen—"

"From the print shop? I remember her. She was the one who usually answered the phone there."

"That seems to be the same one," he confirmed. "She told the interviewer that just two days before your mother disappeared, she saw her arguing with that man in front of the shop. From what she could tell, Mason was trying to get your mother into his car, to go someplace with him, and she didn't want to go."

"Did she hear where he was trying to take her?"

"No, she didn't hear any details. According to the notes, she saw your mother shove him away, then run to her car and drive off. He went the other way, apparently."

Willie leaned over to see the file better. As Jake said, that was all the information they had regarding that incident. Apparently at the time Karen didn't think it odd enough to pay closer attention. It was only after the print shop was informed that her mother hadn't gone to help a relative, but was, in fact, missing, that Karen remembered what she'd seen so many weeks before.

Willie swallowed a wave of angry remorse and shoved back from the desk. "If I wouldn't have left that horrible message at the print shop, maybe Karen would have told someone about this right away!" She stood, emotion threatening to take over. Not sure how to contain it all, she began to pace. "I should have told someone the day after Mom disappeared. I should have called the police! Maybe we could have all started looking for her right then, and maybe… Maybe we would have found her before it was too late."

He rose, and she could feel him watching her intently. "Willie, it's not your fault."

"But it is my fault, Jake! I've been blaming everyone else but it's my fault. I knew she was missing. I knew it wasn't like her to just not come home. Sure, she'd done it before when things were bad, but not for a couple years. She'd been doing so well! I should have known something was wrong, really wrong. I should have called—"

Suddenly he was behind her. She'd been stalking the room, waving her arms wildly, not even aware what she was doing. She hadn't seen him come around his desk to meet her, but there he was, holding her shoulders, making her stop moving and pause for a moment to catch her breath.

"Breathe, Willie. You're going to be okay."

Now that she couldn't rely on angry movement, she felt the tears begin to form. Her eyes burned, and she tried to maintain control. She would not break down now, not after all these years and *not* here in front of Jake.

"I could have helped her," she finally said softly.

"No. You couldn't," he said, his hands warm where they rested on her shoulders. "You had no idea where she was, who she was with. Even if you had contacted someone that next morning, how long do you think it would have taken to locate her then?"

"I don't know."

"Exactly. We don't really know anything yet, Willie. You can't blame yourself. You don't even know what you're blaming yourself for."

"I know that my mother disappeared, and I didn't tell anyone. Everything in my life might have been different if I hadn't kept quiet. Other people's lives, too—my brother, my sisters…and Jess! What if there's a connection between her ex-husband and my mother?"

"I don't know, but I'm definitely going to find out."

"You said he was involved in some drug charges. Do you think my mother was, too?"

"No, the drug case involving him came later. I'm not sure who put the notes referencing that in your mother's file."

She took a deep breath. Being around Jake usually made her anxious, set her on edge, but right now his nearness was having the opposite effect. Maybe it was his words, or maybe that she was just worn out from emotion, but the feel of his hands and the tone of his voice soothed her. She tried to let some of the tension drain.

"You're right." She sighed. "We don't know anything yet, not really. But at least this gives us a place to start, doesn't it?"

"Yes, it does," he replied, giving her shoulders a gentle squeeze then stepping away. "We can be thankful for that."

"Then let's start. Let's go find this guy."

"Whoa, this is one for my people, Willie. I'll have my guys locate him and get him in for questioning."

"But there will be questions from the coroner's inquest, too."

"And if Judge Torres wants to talk to him, he certainly can. We'll let you know what we find out."

"So there's nothing more I can do? I'm out of the investigation?"

"This is your *mother*, Willie! Come on, you know how this goes. Your boss will let you know what he needs you to do for him, and law enforcement will keep you posted at this end."

"But I... It just seems..." She paused, running out of words.

He was absolutely right, and she knew it. She had no justification to involve herself. He'd been incredibly kind in letting her be this involved in his investigation already. When it came to questioning suspects, it was out of line to invite herself. Judge Torres would conduct his own inquest, and Willie would be part of that, as long as he let her. As things progressed, even he might decide this was just too close to her and could pose a conflict of interest.

"I'm sorry, Jake," she said, though it was far from easy for her. "I do know how things work. Thanks for being so upfront with me. I shouldn't have overstepped. I trust you to do everything you can to solve this."

"I will, I promise. I know how important this is for you…for a lot of people."

She nodded. "I should really be home right now, shouldn't I? My brother and sister need me. Maybe I can get ahold of Maggie's parents and talk to them."

"That's a good idea." He seemed relieved she was giving in so easily. She supposed she hadn't given him much reason to expect anything but bad behavior from her.

"It's going to be okay, Willie," he continued gently. "We'll find out what happened to your mom."

She took a deep breath and realized the anxiety and hopeless anger she was feeling had all evaporated. In its place was a strange feeling of…what? Gratitude? No, it was grace. As Judge Torres had mentioned earlier, here she was in a time of need. And here was Jake—of all people—sharing grace with her.

She had to admit that whatever she was feeling toward him in this moment was better than what she'd only allowed herself to feel for the past twelve years. She wasn't ready to call him a bosom pal or anything, but it was comforting to realize that she did, indeed, trust him.

"I know you will," she said, giving him a heartfelt smile. "I have that much faith, at least."

\* \* \*

It was well after dark when Willie finally had time to put up her feet and relax. She'd left the sheriff's office and gone home, but no sooner had she got there than she discovered three messages on her phone with urgent questions regarding preparations for the festival's opening ceremonies. Willie was almost glad to have a couple fires to put out; it certainly kept her mind off her other worries. And Jake Richards.

What had he said today that somehow made her give up on so many years of animosity? She still felt very confused about that. Or maybe it wasn't what he'd said so much as what he *hadn't* said. He hadn't shamed her, hadn't argued with her—not as much as he could have. He hadn't accused her of holding childish grudges. He'd been generous, in fact, despite her sour attitude toward him.

She supposed next time she saw him, she ought to offer an apology. He had no reason to accept it, but she needed to offer one. He deserved it. When would she see him? Tomorrow, probably. If he wasn't involved with the opening ceremony, surely he'd be driving one of the cruisers in the parade. With his election coming up in a month, there was no way he'd miss that opportunity.

The parade was a huge event for the locals. Many groups worked all year to get their floats ready. It seemed everyone in the county had some reason to decorate a flatbed trailer and ride along, waving and tossing candy to children. Willie had spent over an hour tonight making phone calls to representatives from the various church groups, jug bands, high-school sports teams and horse clubs that were expected for the parade. It seemed everyone was ready and eager to go.

At one point she got a desperate call from her office intern, Cindy, who needed a little pep talk just to be certain she'd handled everything correctly today during Willie's absence. It was encouraging for Willie to realize just how needed she was. With everything going on, though, she might have liked being a little less necessary.

She took Timber out for a quick jog through the park, then just before dinnertime Maggie's adoptive mother finally returned Willie's call. Mrs. Westerson was upset to hear that Willie was aware of the troubles Maggie had been having; they'd hoped to keep it all quiet. Willie was quick to assure her that the only reason she knew was because she arrived at their house in the midst of all the chaos today. The two women were able to talk openly about their concerns for the teen, but in the end all Willie could do was offer to be available for the family should they need her in any way. Apparently, Maggie was not interested in learning more about today's tragic discovery. She was *especially* not interested in discussing it with Willie.

So Willie had a quiet dinner alone and tried not to fret. Abby and Mac had been out with friends all afternoon, catching up after time away at college, and helping set up for the festivities that would start tomorrow at noon. When Abby finally arrived home, Willie was thrilled to have her sister suggest plopping on the couch and watching a movie together. Willie popped some popcorn, Abby gathered up a couple fleece blankets and Timber snuggled up at their feet.

It was a movie they'd seen countless times before, so conversation was comfortable. Abby told her what this friend or that friend had been up to lately, and how the town square was looking with all the tents and decorations being set up. Willie wished she could have been there—this festival was such a huge part of her life every year, it felt odd to think that setup day had gone on without her.

"Oh, and I talked to your aunt," Abby said.

"My Aunt Pam?" Willie asked. "Where did you see her?"

"I was at the store, stocking up on water bottles and snacks—you know our young-adult group is helping with the health-and-wellness tent this year—and she was there buying some hardware supplies."

"What did she have to say?"

Willie tried not to show her surprise that Uncle Roy's wife had taken the time to speak to Abby. Uncle Roy and Aunt Pam were not truly related to Willie's sisters and brother. Naturally, they all knew each other, but Roy and Pam were certainly never involved in Abby's life in any way. They could have been—Willie begged them to let Abby and Mac come stay at the ranch, but they simply said it wouldn't be right, since they weren't actually family. That was just one of the many things that had happened over the years to cool any warm feelings Willie might have had for them.

"She was offering condolences on the big discovery today," Abby explained. "It was kind of nice, actually. Usually when I see her, she barely gives me a nod, but today she came right over and hugged me."

"A hug! Wow, that is a surprise."

"She said Roy told her about how you were out walking and found...well, you know. It sounded like the whole thing really affected her. She wants to make sure I tell you she's thinking about all of us during this time."

"Well, that's nice. I'm glad she made the effort to reach out."

"But she mentioned something—they're getting ready to sell the ranch?"

"Yeah."

"But you love that place!"

"True, but it's not mine."

"It should be," Abby insisted. "At least half of it. I can't believe your grandfather left it all to your horrible uncle."

"We've gone over it, but that's what the will specified. Juniper Ridge belongs to my uncle," Willie conceded. "I guess if he wants to sell it, that's his business."

"I still say it seems shady, having people come to look at the property while there's an active crime scene," Abby grumbled around a mouthful of popcorn.

"Yes, but…she told you they had people come out to see it today?"

"She kind of bragged about it. Even with all the 'commotion,' as she called it, their buyer still loved the place. That's why she was in the store today, she said. She needed to buy a bunch of things for all the work your uncle will be doing this weekend. I guess the new buyer wants them to take down a dilapidated shed and get rid of a bunch of old tools and junk in it, or something."

"Oh, sure, they'll put themselves out for this buyer, but anytime we've ever needed anything—" She caught herself before she continued.

It wasn't fair for Abby to be subjected to Willie's bitterness. The hard feelings between Willie and her uncle were not Abby's burden. Willie would just keep her grumbling to herself and pray that somehow she could grow to have a more compassionate attitude toward them. She needed grace, indeed!

"I think we've done just fine without them," Abby said with a shrug. "It's just too bad about the ranch, though. I wonder how much they'll get for it?"

"I guess that's not our business, either," Willie advised.

Abby wasn't ready to drop the subject, though. "It can't be as much as they really want for it, not if the buyer is making them do a bunch of work on it first."

"I'm just surprised Uncle Roy has a dilapidated shed. He's always kept the outbuildings in great shape, but I guess... Hey, look, Mac's home now!"

Sure enough, their younger brother came bustling in, dropping his backpack near the door and giving Timber a hug when he left his spot at Willie's feet to go meet him. Willie paused the movie as she greeted him, asking after his day and enjoying his rambling recitation of all the people he'd seen and how many of the floats he'd worked on today.

When he noticed what they were watching, he grabbed a drink, scooped out a bowl of popcorn from the huge bowl Willie was holding and sprawled in the sagging recliner next to them. He teased Abby about her colorful socks, and she made fun of the knees ripped out of his jeans. It was the very picture of the home life Willie had always hoped for.

She clicked the remote and their movie started again. Abby and Mac turned their focus to the screen, then laughed and started quoting lines along with the actors. They'd done this for years—watched the same movie over and over until they had it memorized. There was just something very comforting about curling up on the couch together, just their little family, safe from the tragedy of their past.

It was true, what Abby had said. They'd done just fine without Uncle Roy. Somehow, God had brought them through all those dark times. Despite the fact that Willie had gotten so distracted that she forgot to notice Him working, it was clear God hadn't left them…not even when Willie felt totally alone.

She closed her eyes and made a promise. There were good people around her, and she would be more thankful for them. They hadn't been brought into her life by mere chance; they were here because God knew she needed them. From now on, she would be more mindful of how it all fit into His wonderful plan.

There was a reason her mother had been found now. God must have some purpose in the timing of all this. The mystery of her mother's disappearance was coming to light, and it couldn't be by accident. Today she'd been led in these first steps toward the truth being revealed. She just had to follow the rest of the way.

## Chapter Eight

Willie's alarm woke her the next morning. After such a pleasant evening, she'd slept well. But now it was time to dive into the big day. She had so much to do for the festival! Thankfully, this would probably keep her far too distracted to worry over the investigation.

By the time she was out of the shower and pulling on fresh jeans and a cotton shirt, she realized that would not be the case. Images and conversations from yesterday kept repeating in her mind—what she'd seen in that dry creek bed, what she and Jake had talked about in his office, the many questions that needed answers. Had Jake done anything yet to find Jess's ex-husband and question him about possible involvement with Willie's mom? Just what role did Uncle Roy play in all of this, anyway? After all, it was his ranch where the body had been found.

*Juniper Ridge.* All of Willie's life, it had been a precious place for her. It was her haven, her daydream, her playground. How did she feel about it now that she knew it had also been her mother's resting place for so long?

How would she feel when it was sold and a new owner came in to take over, to change everything?

As a matter of fact, it was changing already. As Abby said, Uncle Roy was tearing down the old shed and getting rid of Grandpa's tools. Those were things that had been there as long as Willie could remember. They'd been there since…well, since before her mother disappeared.

Standing at the mirror pulling her hair into a ponytail, Willie froze. The comb dropped from her hand as a horrific thought washed over her.

The old shed with Grandpa's tools had been there when her mother went missing—when she died, when her body was left there on Juniper Ridge Ranch. Could it really be just a coincidence that the shed was being torn down and the tools gotten rid of the day after her mother's body was found?

No, it couldn't be. Uncle Roy had been talking about selling the place for months. If he felt the old shed needed to go to entice a new buyer, wouldn't he already have taken care of that? She suddenly found the whole scenario impossible to believe.

What she could believe, though, was that once her mother's body had been found, Uncle Roy might be in a hurry to get rid of some evidence. Could that be the case? Did some of those tools in that old shed have something to do with whatever happened to her mother?

It was far-fetched, she knew that, but not so much that she could just brush it off. As she finished getting dressed for the day, the suspicions circulated in her brain until she could no longer deny them. Uncle Roy's hurry to tear down the shed and get rid of those tools had to mean something. But what? Could it contain evidence to implicate him?

They would never know if he managed to finish his project. Even now, he might be out there wiping out any traces of proof that would lead them to answers. He might be hiding his guilt, and if something wasn't done right now, he could get away with it!

She grabbed her phone and called Jake's office. He didn't answer and she hadn't thought to get his cell-phone number, so all she could do was leave a message asking him to call her as soon as he could. She hoped he wouldn't ignore her, but it wouldn't have been surprising if he did. She hadn't given him much reason to look forward to their conversations.

Well, the next person she could turn to was Judge Torres. He would know what to do. She quickly called his home number.

This time, she got an answer. It wasn't the judge, though, it was his wife.

"*Hola*, Willie! How are you holding up today?"

Elisa Torres was the sweetest, smartest, feistiest ball of energy Willie had ever known. She was just as busy with her work as the judge had always been with his. Since the couple never had children of their own, Elisa devoted herself to the whole county. She ran a food pantry for the church and offered shelter to the homeless. Elisa managed the only motel in town and ran a bustling diner there, too. It had been in her family for generations, and even after marrying a successful young lawyer, she'd kept working as hard as ever, giving away as much as she earned. Mac and Abby had both enjoyed working summer jobs for Elisa.

Today, though, Willie would have much rather been talking to the judge.

"I'm sorry, but he's already gone off to the barber to get all spiffed up," Elisa said. "It's a big day, you know. Is everything all right? Can I help you, Willie?"

"I'm fine, thank you," she assured her. "It's just... something has come up regarding the investigation about my mother. I really need to talk to him."

"Of course. He told me about it—how horrible for you. Come to my kitchen sometime. We'll have soup and you can talk."

"I'll do that, Elisa. Thank you. As soon as the festival is over, I'm sure I'll need a bowl of your soup and a shoulder to cry on."

Elisa promised to have the judge call her back when he could, but Willie knew his schedule today would be pretty full. She hesitated to call on his mobile phone— were her silly suspicions worth pulling him away from his busy morning? He might simply think she was beginning to crack under all the strain.

Still...she couldn't shake the feeling that her uncle's decision to tear down a building and get rid of old tools was just too convenient right now. The destruction could be happening this minute, while she made phone calls and waited to contact someone! How could she sit by?

She wasn't due in town for the festival for over an hour; she could use that time to run out to the ranch and at least speak to her uncle, find out what his plans were. If he truly had nothing to hide, surely he would cooperate, just for the sake of saving face.

If he did not cooperate...then perhaps Willie could consider that an answer to the question about whether he was trying to hide evidence. By that time, maybe she could get in touch with Jake or Judge Torres. Someone needed to know what was happening. They would certainly be interested to learn that Uncle Roy was proceeding with his plans even after being warned.

Mac and Abby were just waking up for the day, so Willie quickly instructed them to take Timber for a walk and give him his breakfast before they left. She thought about telling them where she was going but worried that might make them concerned. At this point, there was no sense in casting more of a shadow over their day.

She left another message for Jake while driving out to the ranch. He needed to know what was going on, even if he might not believe it meant anything important. She drove the familiar roads, only half glancing at the rocky hillsides and dusty trails as she passed by. The scrubby pines, gnarled oaks, spreading sumacs and stately cottonwoods were just beginning to show their fall colors. Soon the hillsides would be awash with orange and gold.

Today, though, Willie's mind was on everything else. Jake would probably scold her for going out here, but she could put up with that. Someone needed to speak to Uncle Roy, and right now, she was the only one available. If Jake got himself here and was willing to take Willie's concerns seriously, she'd be happy to back off and let him handle her uncle.

For now, though, it was all on her. As she drove up the lane and the old ranch house came into view, she wished she had waited for Jake. The closer she got, the more the idea of confronting her uncle seemed like a bad idea. What could she say to him? Did she really expect an honest answer when she asked why he was planning to tear down that shed?

Coming around a bend, she was surprised to see that the shed in question was still standing. She felt a wave of relief. It was set back behind one of the buildings that had been used as housing for ranch hands. It looked like it had seen better days—obviously Uncle Roy had not wasted time and money keeping that shed in the same condition as the rest of the place. It was overgrown with weeds and the roof sagged quite noticeably.

But no one was tearing it down, so at least that was a good thing. Maybe her uncle hadn't been planning to tackle that project, after all. Maybe Abby misheard Aunt Pam, or maybe the work wasn't as urgent as Willie feared. Whatever the reason, it still seemed intact. Perhaps any clues it might hold would still be untouched.

Uncle Roy's truck was in the wide parking area near the house, so she knew he was home. She didn't see Aunt Pam's SUV, but it could have been in one of the garages. Willie eyed the long building that had once been exclusively a garage, but had been partially converted to be Aunt Pam's art studio.

Willie always felt a pang thinking about that. So much of her life, she'd longed for her own space to spread out, to create, where she had room for all the supplies she needed, where she didn't have to fend off the eager fingers of her little sisters and brother, where she could explore working with new materials and creating larger projects. She had longed to try her hand at sculpting.

Well, Aunt Pam had done all of that. Once she married Uncle Roy just before Grandpa died, she quit her job as a lawyer and converted these garage bays to her studio. She filled the place with her work—huge, bold abstract pieces constructed from metal and found objects welded together. She never let Willie work with any of her tools or materials, or even venture inside very often, so the studio had always been a place shrouded in mystery to Willie.

Even now, with no one else around, Willie knew better than to just walk in looking for her aunt. She parked her truck and hopped out, wondering which way to go. Should she knock at the front door of the home and demand to see the contents of that shed? Should she take her chances and sneak out to the shed on her own to snoop around? The idea was tempting...

"Willie!" Aunt Pam's voice surprised her.

"Good morning," Willie replied, hoping to sound cheerful when really she felt shaky and anxious.

"What brings you out here?"

Pam was carrying a box of what appeared to be old newspapers. She'd just come out the side door of the rambling house, and if she hadn't called out, Willie doubted she'd have even noticed her.

"I was just...hey, that looks heavy. Can I help you with that?"

Her aunt seemed more than happy to accept her offer. "Sure! Roy was supposed to bring these out to burn, but you know how he is. Maybe you could grab a stack so this box isn't so heavy."

Willie reached in and pulled out an armful. She was impressed that her petite aunt had been hauling so much. Then again, ranch women were used to hard work. Not that Willie usually thought of Aunt Pam as a ranch wife. No, she'd come from a suburb of Dallas and made no secret of the fact that she missed the convenience and bright lights of home.

"Doing some cleaning out?" Willie asked as she followed Aunt Pam toward the back of the house with her bundle.

"Yes, you know we're selling the place," she said, and was kind enough to sound just the slightest bit regretful. "It's simply too much for Roy to keep up with, and we've found someone interested in it."

"So I've heard. I guess that's why Uncle Roy is getting ready to tear down the old tool shed?"

Aunt Pam looked surprised, then broke into a smile. "Ah, I mentioned that to Abby, didn't I? It was so nice to run into her yesterday! Wow, she'll be graduating from college soon. It's hard to believe!"

"Yes, it is. And Mac's gone off to college, too. I still think of them as little kids, but they keep reminding me they're not."

"That's the same thing all my friends with kids say," Aunt Pam said.

They had come around behind the house and followed a stone pathway down a gentle slope. An old firepit was set up back here. Willie remembered nights long ago sitting around the fire with her parents and grandfather. Sometimes friends would join them; someone usually had a guitar and there was music. Her grandfather had tried to teach her to roast marshmallows on a stick, but she usually burned them. Those were good times, but too long ago. The memories faded with each year that went by.

From the looks of it, it had been years since the firepit had been used for anything other than burning old newspapers. The log benches Grandpa had made were rotted and neglected. The rocks surrounding the pit had weeds growing in them. There were no signs of charred marshmallows anywhere.

"Just toss them in," Aunt Pam instructed. "I've got a few more to bring out, and Roy will probably have some junk from the shed he can burn."

"He's going to be working on that today?"

"I hope so. The buyer wants this done right away."

"So you're sure this person is going to buy the place? It's pretty firm?"

"Isn't that great? Sometimes it can take forever to find a buyer for a ranch like this—mostly scrub land and only a small herd of cattle. Roy did his best, of course, but you really can't make a living off this place."

"Grandpa seemed to do all right."

"Sure, back in the day," Aunt Pam said, wiping her hands on her jeans. "But not now. Roy finally had to admit it."

"Well, you know I'll be sad to see it leave the family. My great-grandfather built this ranch. Are you sure it's such a good idea to sell it? I mean, especially right now, just after…"

"Just after what?"

"Finding my mother's body on the property! Your buyer is aware of this, isn't he? Does he want to buy the place while it's part of an investigation?"

Aunt Pam seemed to shrug off the idea. "Oh, that won't affect anything. It's not like it has anything to do with the house or the actual business aspects of the ranch. It's a nonissue, I think."

Willie was shocked by her aunt's blasé attitude. Finding her mother's body here on the ranch certainly didn't feel like a nonissue to Willie! It hurt her to find her aunt so insensitive about the situation.

Aunt Pam must have noticed Willie's expression. "I'm sorry, Willie. I don't mean that it isn't tragic, of course.

I'm really sorry for you. It's just that I don't see how it has any impact on us, that's all. She's been gone so long... I can't imagine the investigation will take any time at all. I mean, we all know how difficult things were for her back then. It's sad that she chose to end it this way, but at least now you can have closure."

"Wait, you assume she took her own life?"

"Oh, I can see how this might upset you. But Willie, you're an adult now. You can't possibly think there was anything suspicious about her disappearance. It was common knowledge then that she was desperate. You know how she was, a single woman with four kids, loose morals, just about to lose her job—"

"She wasn't about to lose her job. She was a hard worker!"

Aunt Pam gave a sad shake of her head. "I'm glad she managed to keep it all from you, but...well, you were just a child. I'm afraid the truth isn't always easy to swallow."

"How can you say that? My mother wasn't desperate."

"You're saying she just happened to drop dead of natural causes here on our ranch?"

"No, I'm saying that she...that..."

"What *are* you saying, Willie?"

She turned, caught off guard by her uncle's harsh voice. He must have heard them and come out of the house to see what was going on. Willie met his angry gaze as he stalked toward them. Everything about him warned her to stay on guard.

But she wasn't about to back down. "I'm saying there was foul play here."

He furrowed his brow. "Foul play? What do you mean by that?"

"I mean my mother didn't come out here to do away with herself. She did not die by her own hand."

"You think there was some kind of accident?" he asked.

"No, I think it was deliberate."

"What do you mean, Willie?" Aunt Pam asked, sounding genuinely confused.

Uncle Roy didn't let her reply. "She's saying it wasn't natural causes, it wasn't suicide and it wasn't some freak accident. Obviously, she's come here to accuse us of something, Pam. Go ahead, Willie. Say it. Tell us how you think your mother died here on our ranch."

His tone was so cold that she had a hard time finding the words to give him an answer. Uncle Roy had never been her favorite person, but he had taken her in and provided for her. He hadn't been the most loving father figure, but he'd never been cruel or violent, either. Could she really accuse him of such a heinous crime? Could he truly be guilty of—

"Murder," another voice said.

Willie startled, and her breath caught in her chest. She had to raise one hand to shield her eyes from the bright morning sun. In a haze of sunlight and dust, she recognized the man's form immediately.

It was Jake; he had joined them. He stood at the top of the pathway that Willie and Pam had just come down. He must have gotten Willie's message and come out here, heard their angry voices and found them.

Uncle Roy snorted. "You think I murdered Willie's mom?"

"I don't think anything yet, Roy, but I know that's how she died," Jake replied, coming down the path toward them. "We're still waiting for a full report, but they identified her cause of death for certain. It was blunt-force trauma."

"That doesn't mean murder," Uncle Roy insisted. "She could have fallen or gotten washed away in the creek and banged against rocks. How do we even know whatever damage they found on those bones didn't happen after she died? There can't be much of her left to examine after all this time."

"There's enough," Jake said. "The examiner is convinced the huge gash in her skull couldn't have been created by accident. The metal shard found embedded there wasn't from bumping into a rock. No, I'm sorry to say, Willie's mom was definitely murdered."

# Chapter Nine

Pam Henner brought a pitcher of iced tea to the table. Jake had managed to defuse the tension he'd found when he walked up on the three Henners arguing in the backyard and convinced them all to come inside and sit down. Sharp words and accusations wouldn't get them any closer to solving this crime, but civilized conversation might.

He was glad Willie had left a message informing him what she was up to; he'd have some words with her when all this was over. It could damage the whole investigation if she went around taking matters into her own hands. However, he had to admit it was a good thing she'd let him know about her uncle's plans to start demolishing buildings.

"Thank you, Pam," he said as she filled the tall glass in front of him. "It's warming up already today. This will hit the spot."

"Looks like summer weather will be sticking around for the festival," Pam replied, serving the others then taking a seat at the huge table that filled the center of the oversize kitchen.

"With all the festival stuff starting up, I don't see how anyone has the time to be pestering me about what I do to fix up my place here," Roy grumbled.

Willie didn't hesitate before jumping in. "This is a crime scene, Uncle Roy. You can't just go around tearing things down in the middle of a murder investigation!"

"The crime scene—if there is one—is way out on my ranchland!" Roy persisted. "This is my home, and I'm going to do what I like here. Right now I'd like to get it ready for selling."

Willie clearly had a few choice things to say about that, but Jake spoke first. "Roy, you know the investigation takes precedence over all that. I understand you've got plans, and I respect that, but—"

"But she gets to decide what I do with my place?" Roy jabbed a thumb toward Willie.

"As if anyone has ever given me that option!" Willie snapped.

"You have to admit, it does seem a little obvious that no one said anything to us about our home being part of a crime scene," Pam said, ignoring the other two as they fumed at each other and directing her words toward Jake. "There didn't seem to be any problem at all until Willie heard we were moving forward with the sale."

"No problem at all?" Willie said. "We found my mother's body in your creek bed yesterday! How can that not be a problem?"

Jake gave her a warning glance. Her hazel eyes flashed, but she closed her mouth and refrained from further accusations. He could tell she was practically ready to combust, though.

"Look, I understand this is a terrible situation for everyone," Jake said.

Somehow, he needed to find the middle ground for all of them. Anger and insults would not move them forward. He needed to lean on the only thing he knew could bring any peace between them.

"But you three are family," he went on. "You're all hurting right now, which is perfectly normal. I know it's hard to get over things that have been done and said in the past. Right now, though, you've all suffered a loss. Willie is still grieving her mother, and she's desperate to find out what happened. Roy and Pam, surely you can understand that? Kim was part of your family, too. You may have had your differences, but I'm sure neither of you wished her to end up this way."

"No, of course not," Pam agreed.

Jake quickly went on while he still held their attention. "And I know it's got to be difficult to make the decision to sell the ranch after all these years, so your emotions are running high right now, too. Roy, Willie isn't creating trouble just to spite you. It isn't her call—the law decides what is considered a crime scene and what isn't."

"So what does the law say about me tearing down that old shed out there?" Roy asked. "It's an eyesore and a danger for anyone who goes in it."

"I understand," Jake said. "And I don't want to stand in the way of you selling your property. However, I cannot disregard the fact that a murder was committed here on Juniper Ridge Ranch."

"And you're accusing Roy of being involved?" Pam asked.

"No, but someone was," Jake responded. "Until we

can find out who, we can't let anything happen that might slow our investigation or potentially cause evidence to be lost."

"You're saying she was murdered in my tool shed?" Roy asked.

"Can you say for certain she wasn't?" Jake countered.

"Of course, he can!" Pam assured them.

"So that must mean he knows exactly where the murder *was* committed," Jake said, hoping to surprise her.

Pam paused and shared a quick glance with her husband before she continued. "Uh, no, we don't know anything about this so-called murder."

"Then you don't know if the tool shed is important to the case or not," Jake pointed out. "Until we can rule it out, then I can't allow you to destroy it or remove any of the contents. Kim Milson was murdered when someone struck her with a metal object, hard enough to leave shards embedded in her skull."

Jake looked over at Willie. It was easy to get caught up in the job, to focus on the investigation and forget that this was far more personal for her than any other case. He met her eyes, saw the emotions she was trying to hide. She didn't shrink, though. She nodded for him to continue.

He cleared his throat. "For all we know, Roy, that object could still be here, somewhere, on this ranch. What better place to start looking than in an old tool shed?"

Roy's eyes narrowed. "And that's why Willie came barreling over here when she heard I was planning to tear it down and get rid of the old tools. She thought I had something to hide."

"Is she right, Roy?"

The man shook his head defiantly. "No! No, she is not. I had nothing to do with whatever happened to Kim. I never hid anything in that shed, and getting rid of it wasn't even my idea!"

"Whose idea was it, then?" Jake asked.

Pam answered before Roy even had a chance. "The buyer wanted the shed torn down, but someone else had already asked for the contents inside it."

Now that sounded like useful information. Why would someone want to buy old, neglected tools and a shed full of junk? Jake couldn't wait to hear the explanation for this.

"It was Garret Landers," Roy answered.

For a moment the name meant nothing to Jake. Then Willie made a strangled sound and nearly spit out her iced tea.

"My stepfather?" she choked.

"Yeah," Roy confirmed. "He said he'd give me a hundred dollars for all those old tools."

"But…he's been gone for years, no one's heard from him since way before my mother went missing!" Willie said.

"Well, I have. He's been around, and he wants those tools."

Pam seemed just as astonished as Willie. "Maybe he knows something about them."

Roy shrugged. "Maybe he does. I never thought anything of it, but we all know he sure didn't always get along with Kim, did he? They fought like cats and dogs before they split up."

"But he left. Mom had to do their divorce through the mail."

"He sounds like a person of interest," Roy said with certainty. "I can tell you where to find him."

Jake sighed. This was definitely an unexpected lead. At the time of the initial investigation, Kim's ex-husband had not even been under consideration. He'd been out of her life and his whereabouts unknown, according to the report. Everyone they interviewed had been confident he was gone. He hadn't even stayed in contact with his children. The consensus was that he wouldn't have risked coming back to Laurel County because he didn't want to pay child support. The fact that he was back now and showed interest in those tools had to mean something.

Jake checked his watch. The morning was slipping away, and he now had two important leads to follow up on—his ex-brother-in-law *and* Kim's ex-husband. It was going to be an even busier day than he'd expected.

"All right," he said, pushing back from the table. "I'm going to call some of my guys here to set up a perimeter. I'm going to trust you, Roy, to leave things as they are now. Until we can make a sweep of the place to look for anything that might be connected to the murder, you're not to move anything, destroy anything or get rid of anything. Understand?"

"But we've got stuff to do!" Roy complained. "I've got my buyer coming back to go over some things, and I've got a ranch to run!"

"And you can do all that, as long as it doesn't interfere with our investigation."

"But you've got no right to—"

Pam interrupted her husband, calming him with a hand on his arm. "Roy, it's okay. They're not going to find anything, but you've got to let them do this. I'm sure Sheriff Richards will be as quick as he can, then everything will go back to normal. They'll see we've got nothing to hide, and they'll leave us alone."

Roy cocked his mouth to one side and eyed Jake. Jake eyed him right back. He'd never had anything against Roy, but he had no real reason to trust him, either. Their friendship was based purely on the convenience of working together over the years on local committees and the occasional barbecue. If Roy wanted to push this and destroy what friendship they had, Jake wouldn't lose any sleep. He'd just get a search warrant and come right back.

"Oh, all right," Roy said, backing down. "I won't do anything around here until you've made your useless searches."

"Good. Thank you, Roy," Jake said, glad the man could finally be reasonable. Now he needed to make sure his niece could be just as willing to cooperate. "So, Willie, you don't have to worry there's evidence being destroyed or tampered with. Now, can I trust you to let the investigation proceed without further harassing your aunt and uncle?"

"Harassing them? But if I hadn't come over there this morning, they would have—"

"They have agreed to cooperate. Now I need the same from you, Willie."

She glared at him, her anger sizzling at the surface. But she was in control. In typical Willie Henner fashion, she took a deep breath, pulled herself up very straight and removed any trace of resentment or suspicion from her expression. She even smiled.

"Fine. I promise to cooperate," she said.

"You make that very believable," Jake teased. "And

since I know you have some early commitments today, Willie, I think we're done here for now. You go on and get into town for the festival. I'll stick around while my guys scramble up a search team."

Willie wasn't quite ready to give up. "And my step-father?"

Jake glanced over at Roy. "You can tell me where to find him?"

"Yes, I can."

"Great. See, Willie? It's all under control. You can go do…whatever it is you're doing today. I'm sure you're needed there."

He could tell she really wanted to argue with him, to somehow keep herself involved in whatever search he'd be conducting, but instead she gave them all another smile—this one even sweeter than the last. Willie rose from the table, and Jake stood to join her.

"I *am* needed there," she agreed. "Okay then. Uncle Roy, Aunt Pam… I'm sorry if anything I did offended you today. I've been on edge, as you can imagine, and maybe I was a little harsher than I needed to be."

"It's okay, Willie," her aunt said. "We understand. Now go on, you take care of that festival! Maybe we'll see you there later for the parade."

"That would be nice," Willie said.

She gave Jake a quick look. He knew what it meant— she wanted assurance that he was not just blowing her off, that he took her concerns seriously. He nodded to her and hoped it was enough to convey his determination. She might have behaved harshly, but she did have a valid point. A crime had been committed on Juniper Ridge Ranch—he'd been too quick to block off just the creek bed as their crime scene yesterday. Now that they knew there was a murder weapon involved, the crime scene needed to expand.

Willie gave Jake one last saccharine smile, then walked through the front hall. He watched her go and heard the door shut behind her. Once again, he was asking her to leave a place she had called home.

It was no wonder any sort of friendship between them seemed so impossible.

## Chapter Ten

The next morning Jake found himself sitting in his office wrestling with a decision. The parade had gone well yesterday, as had the opening of the carnival midway afterward. His staff were stretched and putting in overtime to keep a presence, but he'd still managed to get a team out to Juniper Ridge Ranch. They sealed off the tool shed until a state forensics team could be dispatched to look it over thoroughly, but an initial search of the home and the rest of the property yielded no solid leads. The tools and implements Roy kept were far too new or well maintained to be suspect. It had clearly been a long shot to hope for a discovery.

He hadn't expected to find much after all this time, to be honest. If Roy or Pam had been involved in the killing, surely they wouldn't have left the murder weapon just lying around. Jake's hope, however, had been that some other party had been involved and hidden the weapon there, unbeknownst to the Henners. If that was the case, the old shed would have been the logical hiding spot. Or so would any other remote spot on the rugged, sprawling ranchland. It was unlikely their search would turn up anything useful after twelve years.

Willie wouldn't be happy to hear that. She also wouldn't be happy to hear that he still hadn't located Jessica's ex-husband, either. The notes in Kim Milson's case file indicated Willie's mother had some sort of relationship with Mason Bannet, but Jake needed to find him to learn just what kind of relationship it was.

Jake was not looking forward to that. His sister had been in her last year of high school, eighteen years old and just about to graduate, when she started dating Mason. That would've been two years after Willie's mother disappeared. Jake tried to remember what he could about Mason during that time, but all he recalled was that Jessica's life seemed to spiral once she was with Mason. Well, truthfully, Jess had been spiraling since her estrangement from Willie. Jess filled the empty space in her life with people who did not have her best interests at heart. Mason Bannet had been one of those.

Since Jake hadn't found him yet, he needed to focus on suspects he *could* find. That meant Garret Landers, Willie's stepfather. Roy had given Jake the man's current location and his mobile number. Garret was working at a ranch in the next county, where Jake would visit him this morning. Jake's dilemma, of course, was what to tell Willie.

His instinct was to invite her to go with him. But was it fair to put her in that situation? She knew details about their life and family dynamics from the past, knowledge that could provide valuable insight as Jake tried to make heads or tails of the man's statements. Plus, Willie clearly had some things to say to him, and she deserved a chance to say them. Was now the right time for that? Did she even want to see the man?

Before he could pick up the phone to dial her and find out, his intercom buzzed to let him know Willie was at reception asking to see him. He left his office and hurried down to meet her.

She was waiting in the lobby area, just inside the security check. He could see her deep in thought, staring into the large glass display that showcased a small collection of historical objects and art pieces. He realized one item had caught her eye—a welded sculpture made in the shape of Laurel County with the logo for their Heritage Festival crafted into it. He'd walked by this case every day for so long, he hardly noticed what was inside. It made sense that this one would catch Willie's attention.

"Your aunt made that sculpture, didn't she?" he asked as he came up beside her.

She jumped, startled from her thoughts. "Yeah, she did. I guess I'd forgotten all about it."

"The tag says it was commissioned to celebrate the 150th anniversary of Laurel County and dedicated at the Heritage Festival that year. It's a nice piece."

"It's not bad," Willie agreed. "The way the metal twists and turns around itself is pretty interesting. I'm not sure she worked enough in this area over here, though. Some of the metal seems…unfinished. Or maybe I'm just overly critical."

"You've got a good eye. If you think it doesn't look right, I believe you."

"Well, you're the only one." She sighed. "My aunt sells her work in Dallas for absurd amounts of money. Everyone seems to think she's a genius."

Jake shook his head. "Even geniuses have flops now

and then. The more I look at this, the more I think you're right. She didn't really finish it. Maybe she was rushed."

"Why put in extra work if you get paid, anyway?" she grumbled.

"It's kind of funny that she quit working for a law firm to become an artist, and you ended up quitting art to work for a law firm."

"That's real funny," Willie said, although the tone of her voice indicated it wasn't funny at all.

Jake supposed he could understand her feelings. She had loved art all through her childhood and into her teen years. He'd seen her work back then, and even at her young age he'd recognized her talent. No doubt it was her influence that encouraged Jessica to pursue art. When everything happened and Willie gave up her dreams of art college in order to care for her siblings, it must have been painful to see her aunt take it up as a hobby.

"Look, I'm sorry to bother you," she began, changing the subject. "You probably don't want to talk to me, but hear me out. I don't know how far you've gotten in tracking down Jess's ex-husband to question him, but—"

"Hey," he interrupted her. "You are *not* a bother. Of course, I want to talk to you. I'm sorry to say I haven't located Mason, though, and I'm not sure I want to ask Jess about him."

"Yeah, I can see that."

"So what did you come to see me about?" he asked. "You don't have any suggestions on how to find him, do you?"

Willie shook her head and turned back to stare into the display case. "No, I don't know anything about him. But I was thinking... I do know a few things about my stepfather. He and my mom were married for more than five years."

"Okay..."

"I know that was a long time ago, but I was twelve when he left. I remember a lot from when I was twelve."

"I'm sure you do."

"I could be useful when you question him."

"Well, actually, I was just—"

"And I might be able to remember some of the people he used to hang out with."

"What I was thinking was—"

"And I can also tell you if he's lying. That would be useful, wouldn't it?" she asked.

"Sure, but I—"

"Come on, Jake. I know you've got his location—you probably already set up a meeting."

"I did. I'll be meeting him this morning."

"So why can't I go talk to him with you? I'll do whatever you tell me. I'll keep my mouth shut if you want... mostly."

He had to laugh at the thought of Willie keeping her mouth shut in the middle of such a sensitive investigation.

She didn't seem to approve of his laughter and scowled at him. "This is important to me, Jake."

"Of course it is. I was just going to call and ask you to come along."

"I know you think that since... Wait. What did you say?"

"I said I want you to go with me," he informed her and enjoyed the puzzled look she gave him. "If you're up for it, of course."

"Is this for real? Or are you just messing with me?"

"I'm not messing with you. I know it's important to you, and I'm sure you have valuable insights where he's concerned. I want you to come with me to see him, if you've got a couple hours."

"What…*now*?"

"Would that work?"

"Well, yeah!" she said. "Absolutely. Let's go. Where's he at?"

"He's working on a ranch in Gillespie County."

"But that's so close! Has he been there all along?"

Jake shrugged. "I don't know. Why don't we go ask him?"

She eagerly agreed. Ten minutes later, she had texted the judge to let him know where she would be for a couple hours, and they were off. Jake drove one of the cruisers, and she sat silently with him, chewing her lip as if she had a hundred things to say but couldn't seem to figure out where to start.

He certainly felt the same way. For too many years he'd seen Willie Henner as a cold, immovable object, the antagonist who refused to see that what he'd done was in her best interest. She'd been the unfeeling friend who abandoned Jessica and left her to end up with the likes of Mason Bannet.

Sure, he'd admired her granite resolve, her perseverance and determination to look after her siblings and create the kind of future they deserved. She worked a full-time job, raised two younger children and put herself through college. How could he not appreciate that in her?

But all of Willie's achievements had come at a cost. Not only had she given up her dreams of art school, but she also hadn't regained custody of Maggie. Even worse, from Jake's point of view, was the loyal friendship with Jessica that she'd thrown away. Willie had never budged, no matter how many times Jessica approached her, begging for forgiveness.

And begging didn't come easily to Jess. Her brain didn't work that way; Jess saw things in black and white. They were this way or that way, but never in the middle. She only knew Willie as her friend. When Willie suddenly quit being that, Jess had no idea what to do. She was very lost for too long after that.

She'd been easy prey for Mason Bannet. She took him at face value when he claimed to value her, to want her in his life. She fell for his lies and resented Jake for trying to show her the truth.

Without her best friend, Jess saw no reason to pursue her own dreams of art school. Mason promised her love and companionship, and that's what she craved more than anything. One week after graduation, Jess took off. Nothing Jake or their parents did could convince her to come back. Not even after they realized just how badly Mason was treating her.

Jake used to like to blame Willie for that. Now, though...he just couldn't. He couldn't help but see her as another victim in a very old tragedy. She'd done what she needed to do to get through it, and now Jess had, too. There was no sense laying blame. All Jake could feel was relief that his sister was in a better place, and appreciation that he'd finally gotten to know the person Willie had become.

"What do you think will happen if you have to bring Jess's ex-husband into town for questioning?" she asked out of the blue.

"I don't know," he replied. "I'd hope nothing would

happen, but I really don't know. Mason loves to manipulate people. To be honest, I'm just worried Jess might let him talk her into giving their relationship another try."

"Poor Jess."

"I just don't know if she's strong enough to send him away again."

"She's pretty strong, Jake. She knows who she is and what she wants in—"

"No," he interrupted. "She *used* to be strong, and she *used* to know who she was. Things changed after you...well, things changed."

"I see." She was silent for a few moments.

He knew she'd heard the meaning behind his words. He wished he could take them back now. He hadn't meant to make her feel bad, but her silence and the way she picked at the fabric of her jeans told him that he'd hit a tender spot.

"Just another thing gone wrong because of me," she finally said. "I made things so much harder than they had to be. I knew Jess didn't have other friends—not anyone close."

"Willie, I wasn't trying to say any of this was your fault."

"But it is. I knew Jess was different from the other kids. When I quit speaking to her, of course, she didn't have anyone else to turn to. I saw her sitting alone at lunch in the cafeteria those last two years of high school. How could I not? But I chose to keep being hurt and to keep hurting her because of it."

"But you were just—"

"I was just a selfish teenager who was suffering, and I think I wanted others to suffer, too. I told myself all the time that everything I did was justified, but it wasn't. I didn't tell anyone about my mom because I didn't want to admit she wasn't there. I abandoned Jessica because I was too stubborn to admit she'd done the right thing and I hadn't. She ended up with someone who took advantage of her because she was alone, and she was alone because of me, Jake. So, yeah, I take the blame."

"Well, if you don't mind, I would much rather keep holding Mason Bannet accountable for his behavior toward my sister. We don't know...maybe she would have ended up with him even if nothing had happened to you."

"How did she meet a guy like that, anyway? Isn't he way older than her?"

"Yes, by ten years. In her last year of high school, she started working at the restaurant that used to be up at the north end of town. He worked there, too. She'd just turned eighteen, and she was flattered that a guy in his twenties would notice her."

"Too bad he turned out to be a loser."

"He'd already had some trouble with the law, and we all knew he was bad news. I tried to tell her to stay away from him."

"I'm sure she loved that, orders coming from her overly protective big brother."

He couldn't help but wince at the old memories. "Exactly. If there is a gentle, productive way to warn someone about their new love, I didn't even try to find it."

"Did you go at her like Sheriff Jake, guns ablazin' with fire in your eyes?" She laughed, apparently highly amused by the mental image she had created.

"Probably. I told her all the bad things I knew about him, that he'd been picked up for drugs a couple times, that he didn't seem to keep a job very long—every red flag."

"But she didn't listen."

"No. In fact, I think it made her more determined to be with him. Maybe she wanted to save him, maybe she just didn't believe me because she'd only seen the good side of him at that point."

"She does tend to take things at face value."

"That's exactly what she did. He had an explanation for every strike against him, and she believed him. He said he wanted to marry her and take care of her forever, and she believed that, too."

"I'm sure your parents were thrilled."

He chuckled at her sarcasm. "They reacted about as well as I did. They told her what they thought of him and refused to support a marriage like that."

"So she ran away with him."

"She did. They went to Dallas and got a place there. My parents figured she'd come to her senses once her graduation money ran out, and then she'd come home. But I took a more proactive approach."

"Oh? What did you do?"

"I went and had it out with him. I told him what he was doing was wrong, that Jess was just a kid and that he needed someone to teach him a lesson."

"You did not!"

"Yes, I did. I picked a fight right there in her ratty little apartment. I'm just happy no one called the police. In the end, it only made Jess feel sorry for him. She told me she never wanted to see me again."

"Ouch, that's harsh."

"We didn't speak for almost two years after that. To prove she was old enough to make her own choices, she and Mason went right out and got married. She didn't go to school in the fall, and he did whatever he wanted while she worked to support them." He paused, shaking his head. "I'd hear reports of them being evicted, him getting caught driving under the influence, and I knew it was bad. I worried he might even hurt her. No matter how many times they argued, she always took him back. My parents were beside themselves, but what could they do? She just pushed us further and further away."

"Did Mason get any better when Shaye came along?" she asked.

"No, but Jess did. Something changed in her when she became a mother. I guess she wanted better for her daughter than she'd settled for herself."

"And you'll do anything to keep her from going back to him."

"Absolutely! The last thing I want is for him to come around and smooth-talk his way back into their life."

"Well, he's a part of this investigation, Jake. You're going to have to find him and talk to him at some point. Maybe you should reach out to Jess before then, to prepare her a little."

He tried to picture any conversation with his sister that involved Mason and didn't involve eventual yelling and her storming off. He couldn't. Even now, this was a topic he and Jess simply could not discuss. Just the thought of bringing it up practically terrified him.

"I'm just so worried I'll say something wrong…that she'll assume I'm accusing Mason of something horrible, and she'll rush back to him to protect him."

"Well, what if I talked to her?" she asked. "We don't have any history about this guy, and it's not like we've still got a great relationship we need to preserve. Why not let me talk to her, find out if she knows where he is? Besides, she should be prepared if he simply shows up sometime for questioning."

He thought about her suggestion. It was a good one, actually. Jess did need to know what was going on and that Mason was connected—even if only in a small way—with Kim Milson's disappearance. She'd be able to get herself ready, take time to process this information and consider a plan should she run into him on the street. Or should he show up at the door and demand to visit with Shaye.

"All right," Jake conceded. "Go ahead. When you talk to her, tell her she can come to me about it if she wants to. Otherwise, tell her I thought she'd want to know."

"Great. Consider it done."

"Thanks. She'll be happy you reached out to her."

"I don't know about that, but I'll be happy. I should've reached out to her a long time ago."

## Chapter Eleven

Willie was feeling hopeful when Jake pulled the car up in front of the office for the Hickman Ranch. It was a larger operation than Juniper Ridge, but only about forty-five minutes away. Her stepfather was probably one of a dozen hands who worked here. It was hard to believe he'd been so close all this time.

"Are you going to be okay?" Jake asked as he put the car in Park.

"Yeah. I'm fine."

"I know you have a lot to say to him—"

"I don't have anything to say to him!" she corrected sharply. "I just want to know what he knows about my mother."

"No, you don't sound like you've got any baggage hanging on…"

She realized his sarcasm was totally justified. "All right, I'm a little bit tense."

"If you don't think you can handle this, Willie, then maybe—"

"I can handle it!" she insisted. "Yes, I do have some baggage, but I'm a professional. We're here to ask him some questions regarding a case, nothing more. You can trust me."

She pulled off her seat belt and was about to let herself out of the car, but he stopped her. She met his eyes and found his gaze full of reassurance.

"Of course, I trust you," he said. "It's not a matter of trust, it's a matter of concern. This might be difficult for you, seeing him again after all these years. You've already had a pretty rough couple of days."

She wasn't used to all this sympathy she was getting from him, and she wasn't sure she liked it, either. It felt too much like pity. She didn't want pity from anyone, especially not Jake Richards.

"Come on," she assured him. "Didn't you say you called to let him know we're coming? Let's go find out if he waited around or took off the minute he heard from you."

Jake smiled, the worry not quite leaving his eyes. But she wasn't watching his eyes. Willie carefully looked at everything but him as they left the car and headed for the office. She remembered the days when her grandfather had a full complement of ranch hands working on Juniper Ridge. They'd filled the old bunkhouse and kept a busy office in one of the outbuildings—one of several that had been sitting empty for the last years. Things certainly were different there with Uncle Roy in charge.

"Did you tell your brother and sister you were meeting him today?" Jake asked quietly as they walked.

"No," she replied, with no explanation.

She would tell them about finding their father once she knew where things stood, once she knew what his involvement was in their mother's disappearance. Once she knew if he would even be here to meet them today. There was no sense getting Abby and Mac's hopes up for the father they barely remembered. He'd already abandoned them once and stayed away all this time. Why even tell them about him if he was just going to take off again?

Jake's boots echoed on the porch as they stepped up to the office door. It opened before they even knocked. A man stood there, obviously waiting.

Willie had to pause. She knew this was him, the man who'd been married to her mother for five years. She'd been taught to call him Dad. His face was familiar, but she honestly wasn't sure if she would've known him on the street. It had been a long time, and she certainly hadn't pored over family photos trying to keep his memory alive.

But he recognized her. "Willemina," he said, calling her by the name her mother had used. "You're all grown up now."

"That's what happens in seventeen years, Garret," she said, then quickly handed off the conversation. "And this is Sheriff Jake Richards. He'd like to ask you some questions."

"Of course. Come on in, Sheriff. You must be Bo Richards's boy, right?"

Jake nodded. "I am. You know my father?"

"He was the only veterinarian Vern Henner would use when I worked on Juniper Ridge Ranch. Is Bo still working at it?"

"He sure is," Jake replied, far too cheerfully for Willie's liking. "I'm surprised you remember him."

"Oh, I remember him. He was a good man, great way with the animals," Garret said wistfully. "Even the ornery ones, fresh off the range. He treated them all real well."

"Thanks, I'll tell him you remember working with him," Jake said with unnecessary kindness in his voice. "He'll be glad to know he made such a good impression."

Willie eyed the two men. Jake seemed nearly ready to slap the guy on the back and invite him over to watch the game. Was he so easily charmed with a few nice words about his father? Why wasn't he taking this seriously, approaching her stepfather with a heavier hand? After all, this was the man who left her mother alone to raise three children and never even bothered to ask how they were doing. It would take more than sweet reminiscing about his time working for dear old Grandpa Vern Henner to make Willie warm toward him, that was for sure.

"It's nice to chat about old times, but we came with some specific questions," Willie reminded Jake.

He gave her a look that said she was supposed to be following his lead. Yes, that was the arrangement, but honestly...why was he being so friendly? This was nothing like a social call, and Garret Landers needed to know that.

Even if Jake didn't take Willie's hint, Garret did. He nodded and invited them to have a seat. The ranch office was a large room at one end of a bunkhouse. There were two desks with computers, several filing cabinets and maps of the property hung up on the wall. Mismatched chairs lined the perimeter. Garret pulled a couple out.

There was no sign of anyone else, so Willie figured the rest of the staff was all out working somewhere.

Garret must've stayed back to talk with them. That was one point in his favor, at least.

"You want to know where I was when Kim disappeared," Garret said, without any sign of hesitation.

"Yes, we do," Willie replied. "That's all we're interested in."

"All right then, I'll tell you," Garret said. "I was in prison."

"Prison?" Jake repeated. Neither of them had expected that answer. "Which one?"

"I'm ashamed to say it, but I got myself into some trouble. It took seven years in Wiley State Jail to sort myself out."

"You know I'll need to confirm that," Jake said.

"Of course, it's all public record. I went in six months after I left Laurel County. I was surprised it took that long for things to catch up with me."

"What things?" Willie asked.

"Drugs, breaking and entering, receiving stolen property—those sorts of things."

"You were doing that while you were still with my mom?"

He nodded, and if she didn't know him better, she would've thought he showed real remorse. "Yeah. I started working for some pretty rough people. For my sake, Kim tried to pretend it was okay, but it didn't take her long to realize how bad things were. I was tied into dangerous stuff, and she wanted me to get clear of it."

"But you didn't want to," Willie added.

"I *did* want to, but I couldn't. I owed people, they started making threats. It got so bad I was worried for Kim and you kids. I didn't want anyone to come after you all, so I left."

"And six months later you got caught and went to jail," Jake said. "I'm not sure I buy it. I didn't see anything about you being charged in Laurel County."

"They didn't get me in Laurel County," Garret explained. "It was in Dallas. Most of the operation I worked for was in Dallas, and they just passed stuff through Laurel County. That was my job, receiving it when it came in, then making sure it got to the right place to ship out. Sometimes I took it to Dallas myself to a drop-off point there. When I ended up in Dallas full-time, that's when I got deeper involved. We were breaking into places then, taking anything we could sell. I was in a desperate way by then."

"Who is *we*?" Jake asked.

Garret shrugged. "Most of the people I worked with were petty criminals. I honestly didn't know most of them. The ones I did were all picked up right around the same time as me. I can give you their names, if you'd like."

"I would like that," Jake said.

He had his notebook out and was writing. Willie wished she'd brought along her own notebook, mostly so she'd have an excuse not to even look at her stepfather. There was something too earnest, too honest, in his eyes for her comfort.

After ripping a blank page, Jake handed it over to Garret. The man nodded and picked up a pen from a cup on the nearby desk. They all sat silently as Garret jotted some names and handed the paper back to Jake. Willie wasn't sure if she was surprised or just suspicious that Garret gave out his information so easily.

Jake looked over the list, but Willie could tell by his expression that none of the names there meant anything to him. That was disappointing. She hoped they'd get something useful from the man who had ruined her mother's life. The least he could do was help them figure out who had ended it.

"None of those guys are from Laurel County," Garret said as Jake studied the list. "I met all of them in Dallas, and they were peons like me. I never did find out who I was working for, not when I was in Dallas and not when I was still home, moving stuff through Laurel County."

Willie was glad to see Jake wasn't about to fall for that. "Come on. You must have had some idea."

"I didn't!" Garret insisted. "It was all handled anonymously. This kid would give me a note with some instructions, all typed up so I couldn't even judge the handwriting. It would give me a pickup location and where to drop off. I'd go move the stuff in the night, and I never saw anyone else. An envelope would show up in the mailbox a couple days later with my payment."

"Where was it mailed from?"

"It wasn't. Somebody stuck a plain, unmarked envelope in the box. I never saw who did it. We needed the money. I wasn't exactly gainfully employed back then."

"You were when Mom met you," Willie pointed out. "You worked for my grandfather on the ranch. Was that just too hard for you? It was easier to quit that and go into crime?"

"I didn't quit that," Garret declared. "No, I liked working there. I met your mom and we hit it off. Seemed like we had it made. I had a good job, and your granddad let us stay in the cabin on the ranch. It was a good thing. But then…"

"Then?"

"Well, I don't like to talk bad about your family, but…"

"But what?"

"Once Kim and I got married, Roy started to resent me. You know, I was only a hand, just an employee there, and then suddenly your granddad was treating me like part of the family. I don't think that sat right with him."

"Or maybe he knew you were bad news for my mother," Willie suggested.

Instead of being offended, Garret seemed to accept her words. "That could be it. I wasn't much of a prize, I'll give you that. If not for those two beautiful kids coming from our marriage, I believe Kim would've been better off without me."

Willie hadn't expected the man to be so honest about his failings. How was she supposed to respond? Lies she could manage…but not honesty. She was still struggling to find something to say when Jake got the conversation back on track.

"So Roy is the reason you left your job at Juniper Ridge? And that's when you got involved in criminal activity?"

"That's the nutshell version, yeah. Roy kept pushing me and pushing me. I think he knew that one day I'd snap, so when I did, we practically came to blows. That gave him all the reason he needed to get me fired. I was too proud to stay there after that, so I found us a place in town and tried to make it work."

"But it didn't," Jake said. "You turned to crime. How long were you involved in this shipping-and-receiving business there?"

Garret scratched his head and took a moment to

think. His eyes wrinkled in concentration. Willie was struck by how old he looked. The years since he'd left their family had definitely been hard on him. It was impossible not to feel some compassion for the man, but she wasn't ready to let herself trust anything he was saying. He'd burned too many bridges for that.

"I did that about three years, I think," he finally said.

"Did you know it was illegal?"

"I knew what was in those neatly wrapped packages, why everything was so hush-hush."

"Drugs?" Jake asked.

"Yep. And I started using the product, too, and that really was bad news. I'll always regret that. One of the packs was open one night, and several small bags spilled out. So I kept one for myself. Then on other nights, too, some of those packs accidentally got opened. I told myself I wasn't stealing enough to be noticed, but I wasn't stupid. I knew the people I worked for would figure it out at some point. Me using was bad for business, dangerous for Kim. At one point, there were some rumors that maybe I took a whole shipment for myself and hid it somewhere. I didn't, but how was I going to prove that? The kind of people I was working for were ruthless. The best thing I ever did for my wife and those babies was getting out of their lives."

Willie choked on that statement. "You think that was *noble*? My mother would probably still be alive if you hadn't taken off like that!"

"I left so she'd *stay* alive!" Garret insisted. "I was dealing with bad people, and the deeper I got, the more danger I put my family in. I swear, I never meant to leave you all in a bad way. I figured you'd be better off without me, that your granddad would look after you."

"My grandfather died, and Uncle Roy only gave us exactly what the law said he had to," Willie informed him. "Which wasn't much. When Mom disappeared, I got sent back to Juniper Ridge, Maggie got put up for adoption, while Abby and Mac got stuck in foster care. Good thing you weren't around then—you might have had to be a father to them."

"I heard about that," he said, his voice cracking with emotion. "It broke my heart, but there wasn't anything I could do. I was sure Vern would take care of you—he wrote up that will and everything. I'm so sorry, Willie."

"You were still in prison at that time?" Jake asked.

"I was stuck, paying for my sins...and I guess you all were, too."

"You said you were in for seven years," Willie pointed out. "In all that time, you never thought to let anyone know where you were?"

"I wrote to Kim once, to tell her how sorry I was about your grandpa and all that, but I don't know if she got the letter. Maybe she did and she just didn't want to reply. I left her alone after that...then I heard she was missing."

"And as far as we knew, you were, too," Willie said. "Why didn't we hear anything when you were released? You could have reached out."

"I planned to!" Garret said, his face brightening at the memory. "I came back to Laurel County, planning to find my kids and do what I could for you all...even that little one who came along after I left. I heard she didn't have a father. But by then I found out that...well, it was obvious none of you needed me. The baby got adopted, you were working a good job for that judge and had your own house by then, and you were raising Abby and Mac really well. I just… I couldn't see how coming back into your lives would do anything but mess things up."

"We looked like we were okay, so you just left again? Without even a hello?"

Willie's voice had started to rise, but Jake gently laid a hand on her shoulder. His warmth and gentleness suddenly calmed her. He gave a reassuring smile that conflicted with the turmoil she felt inside. How could she believe anything Garret said, trust his explanations? She didn't even want to be in the same room with him.

But they needed to hear Garret out. She could do this. Jake seemed to believe she could, and she was determined not to prove him wrong. She pushed back the years of frustration and animosity and forced herself to listen, to find any truth at all in his words.

"I had nothing to offer a family. Roy heard I was free and I guess he felt sorry for me," Garret said. "He filled me in, told me how everything was going so well for you and the kids. I was still getting used to life outside of prison and didn't have any steady work lined up. When he suggested you'd do better without me, I had to agree."

"Oh, so now it's Uncle Roy's fault you didn't even try to be a father again," she said.

Garret quickly disagreed. "No! I won't hang that on him. I'll take that blame. I needed to get myself together before I could reconnect. Roy helped me get this job here at Hickman, and I set it up so part of my pay every month goes to help out the kids."

"What kids?"

"My kids!" he said earnestly. "You, Abby and Mac."

"You don't send us money." How dare he even pretend he'd ever done anything to help them.

"No, I don't send it to you. It's set up to go to Roy."

"You give money to Roy? What are you paying him for, Garret?" Jake asked.

"I'm not paying him nothing," Garret said. "I don't owe him. It's money for my kids. I send it to Roy, and then he gives it to Willie."

Jake gave Willie a questioning look. "You get money from Roy?"

She shook her head. This one was easy to answer. "No. He doesn't send me anything. What other lies are you telling us, Garret?"

## Chapter Twelve

"It's no lie!" Garret assured them vehemently. "Check my bank records. I send money to Roy every month, directly deposited into his account. But he's supposed to give it to Willie, to say it's part of her grandfather's estate. I figured if you knew it came from me, you wouldn't take it."

"Oh, so you graciously wanted my dear old Uncle Roy to get the credit for taking care of us? You know, I might even believe you...if you and Uncle Roy had ever been friends, or if Uncle Roy had ever given us anything."

He looked honestly confused. "He didn't? But I've been sending him money the whole time I've been here. I made him promise to give it to you. I told him I knew you'd use it right, that you'd see Abby and Mac get what they need."

Willie wasn't ready to believe him. She knew her mother had caught him in plenty of lies. Abby and Mac may have been too young to remember much about their father, but Willie wasn't. Why would she ever trust him now?

"Let's take a step back," Jake said, defusing the tension that had been growing in the room. "We can look into that later. I want to hear more about the people you were involved with, Garret. You said some kid was your contact?"

"Yeah. He showed up one day and said he'd heard I was looking for a way to make some cash. Well, I was, so I said okay. It went on from there."

"He knew who you were?"

"And he knew I had a family to support. But I didn't know him…at least, I don't think so."

"You never knew his name?"

"He went by some nickname, something like Mosey. I told the police about it back when they first picked me up, but I don't think they ever found him. I don't know if they even believed me that he existed."

Willie glanced up at Jake. Surely if there was a drug dealer going by the name "Mosey" in Laurel County, law enforcement must've had a run-in with him over the years. But Jake shook his head; the name meant nothing to him. It was definitely a lead they'd have to look into.

"You left because you thought you were putting your family in some kind of danger," Jake said. "Did this Mosey person make threats?"

"Vague threats. He knew I'd been dipping into the stash. He said the whole county knew, the *bosses* knew, and they wanted payback…or else. When my next envelope came, it didn't have my cash. It had a bill for what I owed them."

"And, of course, you couldn't pay," Willie said.

"I didn't even know who to pay! Then Mosey showed up with my next job. The bosses demanded I go to Dallas and meet up with a group of other guys to break into a warehouse. None of us wanted to be there, but we all knew we couldn't say no. They had me going back and forth to Dallas for a month."

"So that's how things escalated," Jake said. "They had you, didn't they?"

"I never knew anything about them, but they knew all about me. I had to do what they said. I tried to keep it a secret, but Kim wasn't a fool. She knew. She told me to quit."

"But you couldn't."

"No. For everyone's sake, I left. When the cops eventually moved in, I got picked up with the others, but none of the top guys."

"So going to prison was a nice break from all your hard work," Willie said.

"I can't say it was a bad thing," Garret said, surprising her again by not arguing. "It got me out of that rat race, got me clean and saved my soul, to be honest. I'm not that same man anymore. I can tell you truthfully that prison was the best thing that ever happened to me. I just wish I hadn't hurt so many people to get to that point. I finally came to know a God who forgives, and I'm so grateful for that, but I know He can't take away the consequences of what I've done. You and those kids have to live with it every day, Willie. For that I am truly sorry."

She honestly didn't know what to say to that. He did sound like a changed man, though she still wrestled with whether or not to believe him. But why shouldn't she? What did he have to gain by telling them this? It would be too easy to verify his story.

If he truly was in prison, as he said, when her mother went missing, then he couldn't have been involved in it. If his story was fabrication, then no amount of lies now would give him an alibi. The only thing that made sense was that he must be telling the truth.

"So you found God in prison?" she asked, making sure he could tell she was skeptical.

"Your mother raised you and the others to have faith," he responded. "She was a good woman and tried getting me to see the light, but I was too bullheaded. It turns out I should've listened. I sure hope my leaving didn't cause any of you to have doubts or to blame God because I wasn't what I should have been."

"No, Mom never gave up her faith," Willie answered, pleased to say it. "She had questions, I'm sure, but she kept taking us to church, saying our prayers with us and teaching us to love, to care about others. That's one thing you never took away from her."

"I'm so glad to hear it. I hope whatever happened to her…well, I hope you figure it out. I know she's at peace now, but I'm sure you kids need answers."

"We *all* need answers," Jake said, shifting back to fact-finding mode. "I know it happened nearly four years after you left, but do you think there's any way your criminal past was connected to her death?"

Garret chewed on that for a moment, then shook his head. "I hope not. Once I got picked up in Dallas, I had no more outside contact with anyone from that life. The guys I worked with on break-ins, they didn't know any more than I did. We did the jobs, then dropped off the stuff at a vacant address somewhere. I never knew who took it after that, and I didn't want to know. It felt safer that way."

"So who was your anonymous stranger in Dallas, the one who gave you your plain envelope there?"

"Oh, it was that same kid."

Willie glanced at Jake, who seemed as surprised by that as she was. "The same? So he moved on to Dallas at the same time you did?"

"I don't know. Seemed like maybe he worked both places, back in Laurel County and in Dallas. We never talked, so I really don't know."

"And he went by Mosey, you said?" Jake asked, checking his notes.

"Yeah, although the cops never found him. You don't know anyone like that?"

"No, not that I've heard of. I can go back through our files and see if he's been picked up for anything over the years."

"That'd be real good, if you could find him. If those people I worked for did have anything to do with Kim… well, he'd be the link to them."

"I'm sure going to look for him," Jake agreed.

Garret checked the clock on the wall. "Well, if you don't mind, I promised the boss I'd get out to stretch some field fence with him. We've got to move one of the herds in a couple days. He'll be getting antsy if I don't show soon."

"That's fine," Jake said. "I know how to get ahold of you if I need anything. Thanks for your time today."

Garret looked over at Willie. She wanted to glance away, didn't want to meet his eyes, but she made herself do it. She wasn't going to shrink from this man, from all the years of hurt and emotion that were attached to him. She looked right into his eyes and tried not to see anything.

But she couldn't help it. She saw some of the same pain she felt. She saw the regret, the years of wishing he hadn't made such a mess of things. This wasn't simply the vague impression of a man who had helped raise her and put a roof over her head when she was little. This was a real person, damaged and broken but still praying for redemption.

He spoke to her, and his voice held all the same things she saw in his eyes.

"Willie, I can't even begin to tell you how sorry I am…for everything. Your mom would be so proud of what you've done for yourself and for those little ones, though I guess they're not so little anymore."

"No, they're not."

"Well, if you want to tell them about me…just tell them I never quit loving them. I'm sorry I failed you all so bad."

"I… I'm not sure what I'll tell them about you, Garret."

"That's fair enough. I've got no right to anything where they're concerned. You know what's best for them."

"Yes, I believe I do," Willie said.

It was odd to realize that, yes, she really did know what was best for Abby and Mac, because she only wanted what was best for them. She could go home and tell them about this meeting today or she could decide not to tell them. Her love and commitment to them would tell her what to do—there was something powerful in that realization.

They left and went back out to Jake's car. Squinting in the bright sunlight, Willie fished her sunglasses out of her purse. Maybe they'd help hide the weariness that probably showed in her eyes.

She pulled on her seat belt and slumped back in her seat to decompress on the drive back to Laurel County.

"You look beat," Jake said.

"I guess I didn't expect him to be so..."

"Repentant? Believable?"

She wanted to disagree, to say that he was the same thieving liar who abandoned her family all those years ago, but she couldn't. Jake would see through that, too. She couldn't deny that Garret Landers was a different man now.

"I wasn't ready for that."

"Do you think he's telling the truth about sending money to your uncle?"

"I don't know. What reason would he have to lie about it?"

"I can't think of any. Unless maybe he knows more than he says, and he's hoping to distract us by setting us against Roy."

"I'm already against Roy," she grumbled. "And you've already got a search warrant to go through his house and all his things."

Jake nodded. "If Garret really wanted to mislead us, why lie about things that are so easy to check out? I can find out about his time in prison with an app on my phone. I can check on that direct deposit he says he makes, too."

"At least we'll know if he's lying about that."

"Maybe the money you get from your grandfather's estate *is* the money Garret was talking about."

"I don't get any money from my grandfather's estate."

"Oh, come on. When he died, Juniper Ridge would have been divided between the heirs, and that would be Roy Henner and you. Don't tell me he bought you out already."

"No, it didn't work that way. There was a will that set up a testamentary trust."

"I don't know what that is."

"The short explanation? My grandfather didn't want the ranch to be divided up between a bunch of different heirs, leaving us to fight over who got what building, which chunk of the land, and all that. He wanted Juniper Ridge protected as one entity, as it always has been."

"Okay, that makes sense."

"So he drew up a will that put the ranch into a trust, which would be assigned to both heirs equally to be managed. In the event that one of his sons passed away before him, then it would go solely to the surviving son."

"Wow, that totally left you out. I can't believe he would do that."

"Oh, he didn't. There was a monetary amount specified for a single payout to any other heirs. I think it was supposed to be my college fund."

"Did you receive it?"

"Yes, my uncle finally gave it to me when I was nineteen. It came in one lump sum, and he made sure I understood that was all I'd be getting."

"It must have felt like quite a lot for a teenager," he said. "You didn't spend it all in one place, did you?"

"I certainly did! I used that money as a down payment on my house so I could get custody of Abby and Mac."

"What about the college fund you kept in that paint case you used to carry?"

Willie turned to look at him. "How do you remember that?"

"I remember a lot of things about you, Willie. You and Jess were friends for a long time."

"It seems like a lifetime ago."

"I guess it was, but I still remember you talking about art school. You were really talented, too. It's sad that you...well, I guess you've done well working for Judge Torres."

"Yeah. He keeps threatening to help put me through law school, but..."

"But what? You'd make a great lawyer. Unless... maybe you still want to study art?"

"No, that ship has sailed. I'm done with art."

"Well, the funny thing about ships is that they don't just set sail once, or twice even. They float, and they come and go all the time. Just because something seems over and done doesn't mean that it has to stay that way."

She eyed him suspiciously. "You're talking about me and Jess, aren't you? You think that since she's back in town, we should pick up where we left off and become best friends again."

"Well, the thought did cross my mind that she could use a few friends," he said. "And you seem to be working all the time and could definitely use some kind of social life."

"What do you know about my social life?"

"Laurel County's not that big, Willie. You couldn't hide a social life if you had one. And I never see you out doing anything social, so..."

"Oh, and you're one who knows about socializing, are you? When's the last time you even took that uniform off? You're on duty all day, every day."

"I think I'll take that as a compliment." He laughed. "Maybe I should hire you for my campaign. I could get reelected as the sheriff with no social life."

She had to laugh, too. Listen to them, arguing over

who had the most nonexistent social life. To be honest, she had to agree they were probably tied in that competition.

"All right, so we're both dismal failures in our social lives. Why on earth do you think I'd be such a great friend for your sister again?"

"Because you're a great person. And…look at us. A few days ago, you couldn't stand to be in the same county with me. Now here we are, taking a road trip together, solving a crime. We even had a very pleasant lunch a couple days ago. You haven't tried to murder me once!"

"Don't think I haven't considered it…"

Now they both laughed. He had a great sense of humor. How had she not realized that about him? She'd actually come to enjoy the time she'd been spending with him. It wasn't exactly social, but they hadn't been all business, either. She'd found him easy to talk to, and even when they disagreed, he didn't make her so angry anymore.

If she wasn't careful, she might start to like this guy! So she figured she ought to be careful. Her life had no room for anything like that, and she was certain Jake Richards felt the same way. Especially about her. It was one thing for him to want her to be friends again with his sister, but he hadn't made any indication that their newfound friendship would continue after this case.

"Don't you think you and Jess could find some common ground again?" he asked, leaving no question about where his interests lay.

"You're worried about her, aren't you?" she asked him.

"Yeah, I am. I've been praying for her to make friends

again. She needs them, needs to feel connected…like she fits in."

"I'm pretty sure I am *not* the answer to your prayers."

"You might be. How do you know that isn't what God has planned?"

"I think it's safe to say neither of us has the answer to that. I believe He does have something planned for Jessica, though. He brought her back here, didn't He?"

"Yes, He did," Jake agreed. "For a long time, it didn't seem like it would ever happen, but He brought her through."

"So I guess we just never know how He's going to work things out, even after we mess them up. If Jess and I don't manage to become close again, I believe God will find a way to fill the gap."

"You're right," he acknowledged. "It's not up to me to decide how God works. But…do you think you could at least stop by her gallery show today and tell her how great the kids did on their projects? I know it would mean a lot to her."

"I was planning to go to the show, anyway. Of course, I'll talk to Jess when I see her there, if she's got time for me. She might be swarmed by other well-wishers and new friends, you know."

"She might. But if she's not, I hope you're there for her today."

"I will be," she said. "And maybe after the show, I'll have a chance to talk to her about Mason."

Just thinking about seeing Jess again gave Willie a sense of hope. That was a good feeling. The smile she offered Jake was very real indeed.

# Chapter Thirteen

Jake had a few things to take care of in his office once they returned. Willie had said a quick goodbye and thanked him for including her today. As emotional as the reunion with her stepfather must have been, she conducted herself well and definitely helped in gathering information. Jake wondered if the man would've been so forthcoming and transparent if Willie hadn't been there.

At least, he was hoping what he'd seen in the man's expression was transparency. It was hard to imagine Garret still hiding things from them after revealing so much. But Jake still had to check. Some time on his computer would certainly fill in a few details about the man and confirm or debunk some of his stories.

As noon rolled around, an alarm sounded on Jake's phone. He'd set it yesterday to be sure he didn't miss the opening of his sister's gallery show. She'd worked hard with those kids and really put her soul into the work that would be on display. He was eager to see the final product.

After finishing up in his office, he grabbed his hat and hurried out. A large tent had been set up in the center of town, and the children's art would be exhibited there. The whole area was decorated with colorful pumpkins and gourds, shocks of corn and potted chrysanthemums in full bloom. He could hear music coming from another tent across the town square, where a band was set up. The Laurel County Heritage Festival represented everything he loved about his hometown.

And now his sister was back here, too. He greeted a few people as he entered the gallery tent. Sure enough, there she was, surrounded by people who eagerly thanked her and congratulated her on the great show she'd helped the kids put together. Tables, easels and partitions filled the area and the whole place was bursting with color and creativity. She'd turned a pretty standard banquet tent into a wonder—the children's imaginations had created all sorts of interesting pieces that seemed to represent every aspect of life here in Laurel County.

And the best thing about it all—Jake saw Willie was one of the people gathered near Jess. She had come, just as she'd said she would. He shouldn't have worried. Everyone knew that when Willie Henner put her mind to something, nothing got in the way. He wondered if she had any idea how much it meant to him that she was reaching out to his sister.

Jessica glanced over and saw him at that moment. She was never one to be very expressive, but he was rewarded with a smile. He made his way to her.

"What do you think?" she asked. "Does it meet with your approval?"

"It's amazing!" he replied, acknowledging Willie with a nod and a tap of his hat. "You've put together quite a show, little sister. Have Mom and Dad been here to see it yet?"

Jess pointed. "Over there. Mrs. Knoppler took them to show off her grandson's pottery pieces."

Sure enough, Jake's parents were oohing and aahing with a friend from their church. Jake glanced at Willie, eager to engage her in their conversation.

"So what do you think of my sister's students?" he asked.

Willie's heaping praise was enthusiastic. "They've done such wonderful work! Jess, you are a great teacher. Everything is so…authentic. How did you manage to help all these kids with so many different projects?"

Jake was glad she'd noticed what he had. In the past, the kids' art displays tended to be many versions of the same project, as if the teacher at the community center gave them one assignment and just supervised its execution. This year, though, it seemed Jess had allowed each child to create their own assignment. It must have taken hours of her time to help everyone craft such fully realized work.

But Jess was modest. She shrugged. "I helped them the way I figured I'd want someone to help me. They don't need me to tell them what to do—they're kids, full of endless ideas. I let them explain their ideas to me, then I help them get what they need to make it happen."

As if it was as simple as that! But maybe for Jess it was. She'd always had her own approach to everything. He'd done her a disservice to be less than confident in her abilities. Maybe she wasn't quite as vulnerable as he tended to think.

"You're clearly a natural at teaching," Willie said. "I'm so glad they've got you working for the arts program. What other projects do you have lined up for the kids?"

Jess eagerly launched into a recitation of the upcoming schedule for her art classes. Willie seemed to understand how exciting it was. Even though Jess's explanation of the various courses sounded a bit dry to Jake, Willie obviously had a fuller understanding of what it meant. Her reaction was animated and encouraging. She might've told Jake that she wasn't interested in art anymore, but clearly by being in this tent, surrounded by so much creativity, Jess's work had touched that part of her again.

"Well, I'll leave you ladies. I need to go mingle," he said, recognizing that he had become a third wheel.

But Jess stopped him. "Wait, Jake. There's something I need to talk to you about."

"Yes?"

Willie glanced at Jake. "If you two need to talk, I'll go say hello to the judge. He and his wife just arrived."

"No, Willie, please stay," Jess said, surprising both of them. "I'd like your input, too."

"Okay," Willie agreed, although Jake could sense her reluctance to insert herself into any family matter.

"I'm not sure what to do," Jess began, oblivious to Willie's discomfort or Jake's concern. "I heard from Mason. He's coming today to see Shaye's artwork."

Jake was instantly furious, though he tried to hide it. "He contacted you? But how? You've got a new phone, an unlisted address. How did he find you?"

"That's not the issue, Jake," Jess said patiently. "He's coming here, and I'm not sure how I should react. I thought if I told you two, maybe you could be here when he shows up."

"You'd better believe I'll be around when he shows up!" Jake insisted. "Where has he been? I've been looking for him for two days now."

"You have? Why?" Jess asked.

Willie's questioning expression became less about Jess and all about what Jake was going to say next. He realized they were in public, and he needed to keep his cool. Jess didn't know her ex-husband was a person of interest in Willie's mom's case. This might not be the best place to drop that bomb on her.

He took a long, slow breath before calmly answering. "His name has come up. In a case I'm working on."

But Jess wasn't going to accept that as an explanation. "What case?"

Now Jake really wasn't sure what to say. There were people milling all around them, children eager for their teacher's attention. The last thing he wanted was to ruin this occasion, but his sister needed an answer. He couldn't lie to her, and now he could no longer wait for Willie to broach the subject first.

"It's Willie's mother's case," he said softly. "I found a reference to him in the initial police report. I've been trying to find him to ask him some questions."

"Why didn't you ask me?"

"I didn't think you had any contact with him."

"Not much, but he's Shaye's father, Jake. I can't just block him out of our lives if he's willing to have a healthy relationship with us. He hasn't been harassing me or making threats, so my lawyer says I might consider supervised visits."

"I didn't realize you were ready for that."

"I didn't tell you because I knew you'd get upset."

"It took you so long to finally break free from him.

Don't you think it's dangerous to welcome him back all of a sudden?"

"Shaye misses him. I don't, but she does, and she's only seven. So when I told him about her art projects, he said he wanted to come see them. I said okay."

"But now you're not sure what to do when he gets here," Jake said with a sigh. "Jess, you should've thought about that before you said yes. It's a bad idea to bring him here. What if he doesn't want to leave? How is that going to look if—"

"I was hoping for some helpful advice, Jake, not for a lecture," Jess said sharply, then turned to Willie. "What do you think? How should I react to Mason?"

"I guess that depends on what you mean by *react*," Willie replied.

Jess thought for a moment. "Hmm, I suppose I mean how should I act toward him? He's not my husband anymore—the papers will be signed next month. I don't think I should hug him when I see him, but a handshake seems too formal. I thought maybe if you two were here to greet him first, I could just…copy what you do."

"You don't want to copy what I plan to do," Jake growled.

Willie's reply was a lot more sensible. She shot Jake a warning look that reminded him his attitude was not helping anyone. Then she offered Jess exactly what she had asked for.

"I think you should be very pleased he's here for Shaye," Willie said. "You could smile at him, to let him know this is a safe place and that you trust him to be on his best behavior. That is how you feel, isn't it? You're happy he's taking an interest in Shaye's art?"

"Yes! I know how much it means to her. I should probably tell him that, shouldn't I?"

"That's a good idea. Do you have plans to see him outside of the gallery? Does he expect to go to your house?" Willie asked.

She always had such a good way with Jess, and that hadn't changed. While Jake got angry and upset, Willie just listened and took Jess's words at face value, without making assumptions. She replied with information instead of emotion. Jake should know better by now; Jess was not one for nuances, and she never played games. If she asked a question, it was simply to get the answer. She didn't have an ulterior motive. If Jess made a statement, it was because she believed it. Too many times he'd seen that get her into trouble, though, and too many times he'd been late stepping in to help.

"No, I don't want him to visit the house," Jess said simply.

"Did you tell him not to visit your house?" Willie asked.

"No, I don't think I did. I should probably tell him, so there's no confusion."

"You get to be the one in charge of the visit, Jess. He's coming only because you invited him for Shaye."

Jess nodded. Just like that, she seemed quite relieved. In her mind, the matter was settled; she was no longer apprehensive about her ex-husband's visit. Jake had his doubts about Mason's motives, but he wasn't going to share them with his sister. She was beaming like she'd been given the answers to tomorrow's math quiz. As usual, Willie had given her exactly what she needed.

"Thanks," Jess said. "Now I won't worry. But I still hope you'll be around. I know sometimes social things don't look the same to me as they do to others, so I'd love a second and third opinion. I'm not sure he just wants to see Shaye's art, but I hope so."

"Me, too," Willie agreed. "I'll stick around and keep my eyes open."

Jess smiled at her. "Thanks. And I know my brother won't be able to think of anything else, now that he's got Mason on the brain. So I feel confident he won't pull anything today."

"You can be sure of that," Jake said.

Willie laughed and shook her head. She must have thought it strange that he still couldn't interact with his sister with the same ease that she had, yet he could tell she was glad he'd be close at hand. They both knew Mason wasn't to be trusted; Jake would keep a watchful eye on his sister and niece today. Just in case.

"Look, I need to go check on the kids, make sure all the parents are finding their displays. You two will be here for a while?" Jess asked.

"We will," Willie assured her. "I still haven't seen everything here. This tent is packed!"

Jess beamed and hurried off in a businesslike way, politely greeting people and straightening pictures as she went along. Jake bumped Willie with his elbow and gave her a smile.

"Thanks for not getting all bent out of shape with her like I did."

Willie chuckled and shook her head. "I thought you were going to boil over there for a minute, Sheriff. Are you going to be okay when this guy arrives today?"

"I hope so. He's not my favorite person, if you haven't guessed. He treated Jess terribly. He ridiculed her for being different, insulted everything she did and made her feel like she just wasn't worthy."

"That's awful! Poor Jess."

"I simply don't want him hurting them again, you know?"

"Oh, I get it. But I have to say, she seems to be in a really good place now. Comfortable and confident. I don't think she'll let him get that hold over her again. And maybe he is trying to change. Maybe he does want to be a good father for Shaye."

"Maybe, but it's going to take me a while to trust him."

"Understood. But don't you think you should trust Jess a little bit? She is truly amazing, the way she's taken charge of her life, got a job she loves, raising such a good daughter…"

"You're right. I guess I keep seeing that troubled teenager who ran off with the first guy who gave her attention. How can I not worry about her?"

"She seems to have a pretty good understanding of herself now. She asked for our help, didn't she? That says she doesn't want to make the same mistakes of the past, that she's trying to overcome them. I think seeing Mason again is going to be a really good thing for her, especially here, with so many people who care about her keeping an eye on things. She'll be so proud of herself for being in charge, and her little girl will have a special day."

Jake shook the tension out of his shoulders and blew out a frustrated breath. "That would be great—if things go that way."

Willie didn't get a chance to reply. Judge Torres and his wife came up and greeted them.

"Isn't this a wonderful showing?" he asked.

"Your sister has done such remarkable things for these children!" Elisa chimed in. "My nephew's boy loves going to her classes. What a blessing to have her back here!"

"Yes, it is," Jake agreed.

These weren't the only people he'd heard raving about his sister. Despite how he'd acted toward her, he was proud of Jess. Once again, Willie was right. He needed to realize his little sister wasn't that awkward, vulnerable teenager anymore. She deserved to have his trust.

"Oh, and I wanted to let you know, Sheriff," the judge said, leaning in to keep their conversation private while Willie chatted with Elisa about some of the nearby displays, "no worries on that search warrant you needed. It's all legal, I made sure of that. Roy's lawyer has already been trying to stir up trouble, but there's nothing he can do except make a lot of noise. It's just a shame they took their business from good, solid local folks and went with that shady new lawyer after Vern died. I could never trust anything they sent up to me after that."

"You don't think Roy's lawyer is on the up-and-up?" Jake asked.

"He's one of those guys always looking for every loophole so his client can exploit someone. You know the type. Makes sure Roy gets away with underpaying his workers, keeping just this side of legal on everything he does. It's savvy, I guess, but it's not right."

"I know the type." Jake nodded. "I'll try to stay clear of him. No one needs frivolous lawsuits or senseless accusations right now."

"That's right. We've got more than enough to sort out. Got that initial report from the medical examiner. You get a chance to look at that?" the judge asked.

"Briefly. Enough to know what we're dealing with."

"It's so sad." Judge Torres shook his head. "How's Willie holding up?"

"She's been amazing, actually," Jake said, his enthusiasm stronger than he'd expected. "I don't know anyone else who could handle all this so well."

The judge clearly appreciated those words. He gave a proud grin and slapped Jake on the shoulder. "She's one in a million, that's for sure! Well look, Elisa wants to get over and talk to Pastor Jeff. We'll catch up tomorrow, Jake."

"Yes, sir. I look forward to it."

Judge Torres and his wife moved away, so Jake was left with Willie. She eyed him.

"What were you two whispering about?"

"Oh, he was just letting me know that your uncle's attorney has his feathers all ruffled about that search warrant. No worries, though. He says the guy likes to make trouble. We've got all our ducks in a row."

"Good. Kind of makes you wonder why my uncle would sic his attorney on us if he doesn't have anything to hide."

Jake had to agree. The conversation had to stop, though, when a large group moved slightly closer to them, laughing and fully enjoying the day. It was a good reminder; this was supposed to be a time for enjoying art and the many talents of their community. Maybe they could shake off the investigation for a little while.

Or maybe not. The group moved away and Jess appeared at his side.

"Just curious, by the way," she began, glancing up at Jake with her mouth cocked in contemplation. "You said you'd been looking for Mason. What kind of questions did you want to ask him? Do you think he knows something about what happened to Kim?"

Jake gritted his teeth, then decided to tell her what he could. She needed to know at some point. Better now, before Mason actually showed up.

"It turns out," he began, "that he and Willie's mother knew each other before she disappeared."

"Oh. Yes, I knew about that," Jess said, unperturbed.

"You knew he was dating my mom?" Willie asked.

Jess shook her head. "No, they weren't dating. Mason only knew her because he used to work with your stepdad."

"Mason worked at the ranch?"

"No, I don't think so," Jess replied. "I don't know if he ever told me where they worked together. But maybe you can ask him. There he is, coming into the tent now."

## Chapter Fourteen

Willie put her hand on Jake's arm, encouraging him to hang back. Jess's daughter had been at a display table nearby and called out happily when she caught sight of her dad. Jake could only bring tension right now, and it would be a shame for Shaye to miss out on the sweet reunion she'd been hoping for.

"Daddy!" she cried, her ginger curls bouncing as she rushed to him.

Mason swooped her up into his arms. It was a precious sight, and Willie said a silent prayer that the man would somehow not ruin this moment for the little girl. She glanced over at Jake and could see he was feeling something similar.

Few people around them took note—there had been so many happy reunions during the last few days as family members traveled home to participate with their loved ones. Willie was glad that for a few moments, Jess and her little family seemed just like all the others. But no sooner had Mason set his daughter back on the ground than his gaze fell on Jake.

Willie felt the icy chill that sliced through the air.

Even Jess, with her concerns about not properly interpreting social cues, must have sensed that. She took her daughter's hand and began leading her toward the area where Shaye's art was displayed. Mason had no choice but to follow. Any meeting between the two men would have to wait.

"I don't know if I'm going to be able to watch this," Jake grumbled. "He's not here to see Shaye's art—he's here to cause trouble. I can see it in his eyes."

"There's nothing he can do here, surrounded by everyone. Take a deep breath, Jake, and think it through. What sort of trouble are you worried about?" Willie asked.

"I don't know. I thought I was worried that he'd make Jess feel bad about leaving him, that he'd come to try to get back into her good graces. But the way he looked at me just now... I'm not so sure if that's all it is."

"It's going to be all right, so keep steady. We'll keep an eye on him. Come on, they're heading over there to the pottery area."

Without really thinking about it, Willie grabbed Jake's hand. She hadn't meant anything by it other than being supportive, but the sudden warmth of his skin touching hers made her breath catch. She almost pulled away out of instinct, or self-preservation, but his fingers tightened around hers and he gave her a squeeze. The simple gesture sent a tingle through her that put all thoughts of Jess and the investigation out of her head. She was only aware that she held Jake's hand and that he grasped hers back. It was an accidental, casual action that somehow made the world stop around them.

All she could do was freeze in her steps and blink up at him. He looked down and smiled. Neither one seemed in any hurry to let go. Though the moment probably only lasted a heartbeat, for Willie, it seemed to change everything.

"Thanks," he said finally, giving one last squeeze. "You always were the levelheaded one. You're right. I'll keep calm and we'll watch."

"Okay" was all she could utter as she struggled to put herself back into the real world.

What on earth had just happened? She knew she'd been feeling less and less of her old animosity toward Jake, but how could that have so quickly blossomed into something far more amicable? Not only did she no longer resent him, but she also felt all sorts of warm fuzzy feelings for him! Where did those come from?

It was going to take some time to process all this. She wasn't going to get that time, though. Jake's hand dropped away from hers and his voice brought her back to the present.

"Hey, look," he said, pointing to the far side of the gallery tent. "Isn't that your little sister, Maggie?"

She followed his gaze. Sure enough, there was Maggie, looking like she felt out of place in this sea of happy festival-goers and fawning art lovers.

"Yeah, that's Maggie," she confirmed. "I guess she was feeling up to coming out today. That's good."

"She looks like she could use a familiar face," he said, nudging her. "I'll be all right now, I promise. Why don't you go talk to her?"

"What...*now*?"

"Why not? I'll supervise my ex-brother-in-law. You should go check in with her, let her know you've been thinking of her."

She tried to come up with an excuse, but there wasn't

one. She probably should be glad for a reason to take a break from Jake right now—all this newfound goodwill between them was getting a bit confusing. Besides, she did want to connect with Maggie.

Thanking Jake for the encouragement, she left his side and headed toward her sister.

"Hey, Maggie," she said, coming up to the girl.

Maggie jumped. "Oh, hi, Willie."

"How are you doing? I'm glad you could come today."

"My parents made me. They said I had a commitment, so here I am."

Maggie's gaze darted around, landing on everything but Willie.

"How's your friend doing? That must have been scary for you. I heard she was taken to the hospital."

Maggie simply shrugged. "She's fine. I'm fine. Everything's fine."

Okay, so clearly Willie would have no success with that line of conversation. She tried another approach.

"Um, have you run into Abby and Mac? They're at the festival. Seems like a while since the whole family has been together, huh?"

"My family says I'm not allowed to leave the gallery tent. Sorry."

Willie winced at her phrasing. "All right. Can I get a photo of you with your work? Maybe you could text it to them."

"My parents took away my phone."

"Oh." *This was not going well.* "Why don't you show me your artwork—I'd really love to see it."

Maggie seemed hesitant, but after a moment she sighed and led Willie to a display of charcoal drawings.

The largest piece there was Maggie's. It was a highly detailed still life of a collection of children's toys. One in particular caught Willie's eye.

"I recognize that! Isn't that your little polka-dot hippo?"

Maggie brightened slightly. "I've had that since I was little. You remember it?"

"I do! I got that for you after…on your next birthday after Mom died."

They both stood silently for a moment, staring at the artwork and feeling lost in their memories. Willie wished she could reach out and take Maggie's hand or put her arm on her shoulder. She knew better than to try.

"I heard you found her," Maggie said quietly. "That must have been hard."

"At least we can all get some closure now. How do you feel about it?"

"I'm not sure. I don't know what I feel. Everything is just…weird."

"It certainly is." Willie nodded, feeling a connection with Maggie that she hadn't felt in years.

They were quiet again, then Maggie offered a welcome distraction. "Do you want to see my pottery?"

"Absolutely!"

She followed Maggie to a table where clay sculptures and pottery pieces were displayed. For several wonderful moments her little sister brightened and talked to her more than she had in months, explaining how she'd crafted each piece, answering Willie's questions and happily discussing the glazes she'd used and the techniques she'd employed. They moved on to find that Maggie had several paintings in the show as well.

"I didn't realize you knew so much about art," Maggie finally said.

"And I didn't realize you were so talented!" Willie countered. "I guess I should have been paying more attention."

"Well, I never let people see my work, not until I got into classes with Ms. Jessica. She's been amazing."

"Yes, she is."

"You used to be best friends with her?"

Willie nodded. "For most of our childhood. She was always a great artist, even then. We'd sit around drawing or painting together all the time."

"That's cool. None of my friends are into stuff like that."

"I'm sure you're making friends in those art classes, aren't you?" Willie asked, amazed that Maggie was finally opening up to her.

"I've gotten to know a couple people. They seem okay."

"Well, anytime you want someone to paint with, just let me know. I've still got supplies left from when Abby and Mac were younger. I'm sure I haven't forgotten everything about art."

"Abby and Mac liked to paint, too?"

Willie smiled, recalling the messes they used to make and how she'd been frustrated when they were younger. She'd give almost anything to go back to those days and join in with them instead of simply trying to be the responsible adult.

"Yes, Mac more than Abby, I think. I guess it's a family trait we share."

"Cool," Maggie said thoughtfully. "I don't have a lot

in common with my parents. You know, my adoptive parents, I mean."

"I know what you mean," Willie assured her. "And, yes, they're your parents, Maggie. It's okay to call them that."

"It doesn't make you feel…left out? Since we're sisters and all, but they're not your parents."

"They're the people who raised you, and they love you so much. I hope your mother told you I called the other day? I know you've been going through a rough time. If you ever need someone to talk to, I'm here."

Maggie was staring at the ground, fidgeting. But Willie knew she was listening, and they were connecting.

"I know. Thanks," Maggie said. "And… I'm totally sorry about our real mom. Whatever happened must have been pretty awful."

"I'm glad we can finally know the truth. At least, that's what we're trying to find."

Maggie sighed. "I don't remember her, you know? But I always felt bad that she left me…left us. Now I guess we found out that she didn't leave us. Someone killed her. You're working with the sheriff to figure out who did it?"

"I am. And he's pretty good at his job. He'll figure it out."

"Good. I feel like all my life I've had these missing puzzle pieces," Maggie said. "I don't look like the rest of my family, I've got a brother and sisters who I only see on special occasions, my Westerson cousins are all supergood at sports and I still want to duck when it's my turn in volleyball. You know I made the team? But I don't even like volleyball! I just wish I fit in. Maybe if they can figure out what happened to our mother, that will put some of the pieces together."

"I know exactly what you mean. I've been trying for a long time to fit in, to do all these things to measure up to what I'm supposed to be. But really, the best thing I can be is just the person I am...and that includes being your sister. If I'm not too old and uncool."

Maggie giggled and leaned in just enough to bump her with her shoulder. "Naw, you're cool enough. I'm glad you're my sister. Sorry I've been kind of lame."

"It's okay. But be prepared for me to go all big sister on you if I find out you're still getting into trouble."

She worried this might have crossed the line and damaged the tenuous bond she was trying to build here, but Maggie just laughed at her.

"No problem! I'm grounded for forever now, so there's not a lot of trouble I *can* get into."

"Good. Maybe Abby and Mac and I can spring you from your cell and have you over for dinner before they head back to school."

"I'd like that."

Willie resisted the urge to hug the girl. She knew that really would be pushing it too far, but she could barely contain her joy. This impromptu meeting here in the gallery tent had gone better than she could have ever hoped. What a blessing! God truly did work in mysterious ways.

Maggie's parents appeared then, and Willie had a short, pleasant chat with them. They were so proud of their adopted daughter. It was great to see that Maggie was truly in good hands. She'd made some mistakes and she'd probably make a few more, but her parents were keeping her safe. They loved her completely, and she would be all right.

Willie let them get back to enjoying their day and was still smiling when she looked around for Jake. There was no sign of him or Jess, Shaye and Mason in the gallery tent. Willie suddenly felt cold inside. What if something had happened? She'd assured Jake everything would be all right. What if she'd been wrong?

Jake wasn't happy when Mason took Jess by the arm and led her out of the gallery tent. Things had seemed to be going fine for a while. Mason did his duty and pretended to be a doting father, but soon Jake could tell he was feeling bored or maybe anxious. The instant Jake was approached by a festival-goer asking for directions to the historical society, Mason must have sensed his chance. He was already guiding Jess and Shaye away when Jake looked back at them.

And he couldn't tell from Jess's reaction if she was going willingly or if Mason was in some way coercing her. Poor little Shaye seemed to have no idea of the tension surrounding her, so she skipped along beside them. Jake clenched his jaw and followed.

He left the tent just in time to catch a glimpse of Mason—now pulling Jess by the arm—ducking behind the back of the health-and-wellness tent that was set up nearby. Jake increased his pace.

"No, we're not leaving with you, Mason." It was Jess, her voice still calm, but firm.

"Come on, Shaye wants us to be together again," Mason responded.

"Well, I don't," Jake said as he rounded the corner to face them. He made sure the threat in his voice came through loud and clear.

"Stay out of this, Jake. This is a family matter," Mason hissed.

"This *is* my family," Jake declared. "You're supposed

to be here to admire Shaye's artwork, not harass my sister again."

"It's none of your business," Mason growled. "I *did* admire her work. How long does it take to look at some finger paintings by a seven-year-old? Now come on, Jess. You've had your fun, but it's time to go."

"No, Mason," Jess repeated. "I'm not going. I allowed you to visit, but now it's time for you to leave."

He jerked Jess violently. Before Jake could lunge forward to protect his sister, Shaye threw herself at her father. It broke Jake's heart to see the child feel like she had to defend her own mother this way.

"Stop it, Daddy!" she cried. "Don't hurt Mommy!"

Mason had the good sense to let go. He stepped back, almost as if afraid of the little girl. Perhaps he still had enough of a conscience to realize what he was doing, or perhaps he was so much of a bully that he couldn't take a rebuke from anyone, even a helpless child.

He sneered at Jake, then rolled his eyes as Jake felt someone else join them. It was Willie, suddenly at his side, lightly panting as if she'd just run all the way out here. He wasn't surprised in the least—of course, he could trust her to show up when she was needed.

"It's the famous Willie Henner," Mason snarled. "Jess kept photos of you, but it's good to finally meet you in the flesh. I got sick to death of hearing all about you over the years."

The tension halted as Willie looked toward Jess. "You told him about me?"

"Of course," Jess simply replied, clutching her child safely at her side. "You were my best friend."

Mason glared at them. "Some friend. Where have

you been all this time, Willie? But I'm supposed to offer condolences, aren't I? Your mother just turned up."

"How do you know about that?" Willie asked.

"Jess texted me that you found her remains a couple days ago."

Jake realized this could explain why Mason was suddenly so keen on showing up to act like a father again. Jess had mentioned the discovery on the ranch... Did Mason know something that might bring him rushing back here?

"You thought you'd come back and see what else we'd been solving, did you?" Jake asked.

Mason shook his head a little too defiantly. "No, I came back for my family, that's all. I don't care about some old bones you found in a creek bed."

"How'd you know about the creek bed?" Jake asked. "Ever visit there with Willie's mom?"

"Don't go making stuff up," Mason said. "I didn't even know the woman."

But Jess seemed confused. "Sure you did," she said with a frown. "Don't you remember? You told me you worked with her husband and that's how you met her. You said after he was gone, you tried to find him to catch up, so you went to her place to see if she knew where he was."

"Yeah, okay, maybe I did. But so what?"

"We have reports that you were seen meeting her several times," Jake said. "In fact, Mason, you were seen arguing with her just a few days before she went missing. What was that all about?"

"You *argued* with her?" Jess exclaimed, in a rare show of emotion. "About what?"

Mason shook his head. "Those reports are wrong.

I hardly knew her. I asked about her husband, she told me he was in prison, and that's all we talked about."

"My mother *knew* where he was?" Willie asked.

"Your mother knew a lot of things," Mason grumbled.

"I thought you didn't know much about her?" Jake said. "Come on, Mason, level with us. What was going on between you and Willie's mother, and what were you involved in with her stepdad?"

"We weren't involved in anything. I barely ever talked to him."

Again, Jess tried to set the record straight. "Sure you did. You told me about that one time he owed you money, and instead of paying you, he offered to take you to the ranch and show you how to break into the safe there."

Mason looked a little panicked by now. "No, that isn't true. He never said anything about that."

But Jess wasn't backing down. "You told me exactly what he said. 'Come on Mose, let's go out to the ranch and help ourselves to Roy Henner's safe.' I remember what you told me."

"Shut up!" Mason yelled. "And quit remembering things! I swear, Jess, you're impossible."

Willie was standing very close to Jake now. He felt her go tense. She'd heard the same thing he had.

"My stepfather called you *Mose*?" she asked slowly.

"It's short for Mosey," Jess said. "That was his nickname. But I didn't like it, so I never called him that."

"It's not my name!" Mason said, continuing to vehemently deny everything.

Jake had heard enough. "Jess, I think you and Shaye should probably go back to the gallery. Now."

Shaye was already clinging to her, frightened by the outburst, so Jess nodded. "Come on, Shaye. Uncle Jake needs to talk to Daddy for a while longer."

Jake watched them go, Jess still nervous with a protective grip on Shaye's little hand. Their wonderful day had been ruined. Mason had proven himself just as useless as Jake feared.

"I've got nothing to say to you, Jake," Mason said. "I'm done here."

"No, you're not. How dare you treat your ex-wife and daughter that way and lie to all of us? You didn't come back for the art show, so why are you here? What is it about Kim's body being found that convinced you to come back?"

"Nothing. I don't care anything about that."

With Jess and Shaye out of view, Jake took a step toward Mason. They were boxed in behind rows of canvas-covered booths, and Mason found himself backed up against the rear of the wellness tent. There was nowhere for him to go. Like a cornered animal, he lashed out.

Jake dodged his first swing, but Mason was quick. He caught Jake square on the jaw with his next one. But Jake hadn't spent his youth helping his father medicate unruly range animals to let a simple punch from his bullheaded ex-brother-in-law put him down. He whirled on Mason and had the man's arm pinned to his back in one swift move. A quick grab pinned his other arm to his side before he could pull away.

"Get off me!" Mason yelled. "I'll have you in court!"

"Oh, you'll see me in court, all right," Jake growled in his ear.

He glanced around to make sure Willie was out of

danger should Mason break free, but suddenly two armed deputies were rushing to assist. He had no idea where they came from, but he was glad to see them. They took Mason in hand and allowed Jake to collect himself.

Willie stood nearby, her face white with worry. Around the corner of the tent, a small group of on-lookers gaped in shock. At the front of the crowd was Willie's sister, Abby. She gave a sheepish little wave.

"What are you doing here?" Willie asked her, still sounding breathless.

"I've been working here all day," Abby said, indicating the booth they'd been standing behind. "It's a tent. We could totally hear everything you guys were saying. When things started to get loud, I was worried, so I called the cops. You're welcome."

"We were just around the corner when the call came," one of Jake's deputies said. "You doing okay? Looks like he clocked you."

"I'm okay," Jake assured them, rubbing his chin. "He's a lightweight. Get the cuffs on him and let's take him in."

Willie still looked a little shaken, but she managed a smile. Jake gave her one back, though it hurt a bit. He smiled over at Abby, too. Just like her big sister, step-ping in to save the day.

# Chapter Fifteen

❧

"**O**uch!" Jake winced as Willie pressed the ice pack to his face.

"Hold still," she admonished. "It's going to swell up and get all bruised if you don't ice it."

"It's already swollen," he said, but he welcomed her assistance.

He and his deputies had hauled Mason back to the sheriff's office to process him. Needless to say, he wasn't going anywhere for a while. Despite the swollen jaw, Jake was more than happy to have a reason to keep Mason safely locked up. He also didn't mind that he was getting endless sympathy from Willie as she tended to him here in his office.

"You made sure Jess and Shaye were okay?" he asked, although he knew she had. Willie always took care of everything.

"They're fine. Shaye didn't see anything once they went back inside the gallery tent, so that's good. They were going to finish up the show, but I told Jess to text me when they get back home. I assured her Mason's out of commission, so they don't have anything to worry about."

"I'm glad Shaye didn't have to see me leading her father away in handcuffs. That's an image she doesn't need in her mind."

Willie chewed on her lip before finally asking her next question. "She told Mason not to hurt Jess. Has she seen that before?"

"I know he's threatened. It's good to see Jess standing so strong against him."

"Yes, it is."

Willie was silent then, and Jake could practically see the wheels turning in her head. What was she thinking? Trying to determine how Mason's connection to both her mother and stepfather fit into things? Jake still couldn't believe he'd never heard that Mason had a nickname. Now that they had that detail, he wasn't sure if it brought them closer to solving the case, or if it merely begged more questions.

"So Mason is Mosey," Willie said finally. "I certainly didn't see that coming."

"Me, either," Jake agreed. "Once again, if I had trusted Jess a little more and gone to her when we were first interested in questioning the guy, she might have supplied all the information we needed to pull these threads together."

"I wish we *could* pull these threads together, but what does it all mean? Obviously Mason worked for the people who pulled my stepdad into crime. But why would he have been seen several times with my mother? And did she really know where Garret was? She certainly never mentioned that to me."

"You were just a kid, though," Jake pointed out. "If she *did* know he was in prison, are you sure she would have told you?"

"No, maybe not. Clearly we need to talk to Garret again. He must know more than he's telling us."

"That's what I was thinking. I'll call him and set up another meeting. What about you? What's on your schedule for the rest of the afternoon?"

She glanced at her watch. "Well, for what's left of it, I should probably go check in with the festival board. I feel like I've left everyone else to do my job this weekend."

"It looks to me like you already did your job, and all they're doing is making sure things go according to your plans."

"Well, that's the goal. You know how plans are, though. They have a way of falling apart when you least expect it."

Jake laughed and was just about to reassure her when Judge Torres poked his head into the room. The guy was a sight for sore eyes. Jake had been thinking up a list of questions he wanted to ask him.

"That's why you've got to have a Plan A, a Plan B and a Plan C," the judge said with a teasing wink. "And then you've got to be ready to come up with Plan D when all of those fail."

"So what plan are we on right now?" Willie asked him. "How are things going at the festival?"

"Willie, my dear, you are the exception to the rule. We're still running on Plan A, and you are to be commended."

Jake wasn't surprised to hear this, but Willie seemed uncertain. She wrinkled her nose and brushed off the compliment.

"The weekend isn't over yet. I hope we don't have to

drag anyone else from the festival into jail. You heard about what happened earlier?"

The judge nodded. "I sure did, and that's why I'm here. Wanted to make sure the sheriff isn't any worse for the wear."

"Just my ego," Jake said, moving the ice pack so the judge could see his face. "Willie's determined that frostbite will keep it from swelling."

"Hey, I'm only thinking of your public image," she said with mock indignation. "You've got an election coming up, if you recall."

"You don't think the rough-and-tumble look will add to my appeal?"

"Sure, for twelve-year-old kids who like action-hero movies."

"Well, all right, then! I'm an action hero!"

They laughed again, and Judge Torres slapped Jake's back. "You *are* a hero, Jake. It was quick thinking, what you did today. That could have been a nasty situation if you hadn't seen him trying to take Jessica and her little girl away."

"I wasn't letting that guy out of my sight," Jake said. "The real hero was Willie. She found us out there just in time to divert Mason's attention from Jessica and Shaye. She got him talking about the case, in fact."

"I'm glad it worked out so well. You've got Mason Bannet locked in your holding cell, waiting to sing his heart out for you."

"If he'll sing for us." Jake sighed. "He's already law-yered up, I'm told."

"Yes, his attorney is down there with him now. That's where I just was, and why I came up here to see you," Judge Torres said pointedly. "It seems to me that boy does indeed match the descriptions of our mysterious Mosey."

"Interesting, huh?"

"And there's something even more interesting than the man's alias."

"What's that?" Jake and Willie both asked at the same time.

"Who his lawyer is."

"His lawyer?" Jake asked.

"Dale Stackler."

Jake waited for the name to mean something. It didn't; he was certain he'd never heard it before. Turning to Willie, he could see she was also confused. Why should this name be important to them?

"Dale Stackler," the judge repeated. "You know, that slick lawyer from Dallas who handles all of Roy Henner's things."

Now the name suddenly *did* mean something. Jake dropped the ice pack and gave Judge Torres his full attention.

"Why would Mason be using the same out-of-town lawyer Roy Henner uses?"

The judge cocked an eyebrow and leaned against the doorframe. "*Now* you see how interesting it is."

"It can't be a coincidence," Willie said. "He must be working with them in some way! He must have called Roy when he got arrested, and Roy called his lawyer."

"That's what I'm wondering," the judge said. "There's something going on there."

"Let's check," Jake said, turning to his computer and pulling up the system.

Sure enough, there was a record of Dispatch connecting a call for Mason Bannet. He could see that the number went to...the law office of Dale Stackler.

"Huh. He called the lawyer direct," he announced.

"What? That can't be right," Willie said, leaning over his shoulder to double-check.

He cleared his throat to remind her that technically, that wasn't allowed. She stepped back, but she'd seen enough. Obviously, Mason had his own connection to this high-dollar lawyer. But what could it be?

"Maybe it is just a coincidence," the judge said with a sigh. "A mighty big one, but Stackler's office is in Dallas, and we know Mason's from Dallas. Maybe that's all there is to it?"

"I can't believe that," Jake said, shaking his head. "There's got to be a connection."

"Why don't we go ask him?" Willie said. "If he tries to avoid answering or gives some unbelievable story, then at least we'll know they're hiding something. If it is just a weird coincidence, then what motive would either of them have not to tell us the truth?"

She had a point. Jake knew he wasn't in any mood to confront Mason again, but he'd see if he could get a word with the attorney. He called down to the deputy assigned to their holding area and asked him to send up the lawyer to speak with him. The man said he would; it appeared he was just finishing with Mason now.

"Seems you've got quite an investigation going here," Judge Torres said. "Looks like it's starting to involve everyone in Laurel County. You think this lawyer connection really ties him into what happened out there?"

"It certainly connects him to something," Jake said. "And the fact that Mason is actually the kid who was the contact person for Garret...well, Garret wasn't working here on the ranch at that point, so I don't know how that ties in, either. It sure is a mystery how any of these things add up to Willie's mother's murder."

"I'm looking forward to the analysis on those metal shards they found in her skull," Judge Torres said, then glanced quickly at Willie. "Oh, I'm sorry, Will. Here I am going on as if this is just another case. Are you okay, or would you rather we don't discuss details like that?"

"I'm fine," she replied. "I'm as eager as you to find out anything we can. Maybe if we get an idea what the murder weapon was, we'll be closer to figuring out who wielded it."

"Or what we're looking for," Jake said. "Our guys executing that search warrant could have already found the murder weapon in plain sight and not had any idea."

Willie sighed, shaking her head. "It's been so long... I honestly don't know how we're going to find anything. I sure would hate to think my mom's case might go unsolved forever."

"Now, now," Judge Torres said, moving to Willie's side to encourage her. "You're working with the best here. Our sheriff is going to get this. I know he will."

Jake wished he could feel so confident. It was true he'd already turned up a lot of unexpected information related to the case, but he couldn't make heads or tails out of it yet. What if he let Willie down? It was the last thing he wanted to do. She deserved to know the truth, and he would really love to be the one who helped her find it.

The doorway was filled again. Jake glanced up to find a man scrutinizing him. He wore an expensive suit with polished cowboy boots and an immaculate Stetson hat.

"You Sheriff Richards?" the man asked.

"I am," Jake replied. "Are you Mr. Bannet's attorney?"

"Dale Stackler. They told me you wanted to see me? I've only got a couple minutes, but if you're going to try to intimidate me with some bluster about how you're throwing the book at my client for decking you, I want you to know we've got a good case to say he was provoked. I understand you've had it in for him quite a while now. Would you say you don't even like my client?"

"I would say I'm here to uphold the law, whether or not I like the people breaking it," Jake replied. "Sit down, Mr. Stackler, I've got a couple questions for you."

The attorney made a show of checking his watch. "I'd prefer to stand."

"Suit yourself," Jake said, swiveling in his chair and making his own show of leaning back and propping his well-worn boots up on his desk. "I want to know how you came to be associated with Mr. Bannet. Have you been his lawyer for a while now?"

"I'm not on his retainer or anything like that."

"So he called you out of the blue today, and you showed up here within an hour of his call. How exactly did you do that if your office is in Dallas?"

"I was not in Dallas when he called my office. They relayed his message, and I came right over."

"I see. Where were you coming from?"

"I don't believe that's relevant to this case, Sheriff. Try harder."

"Why did Mason call you specifically?"

"You threw him in jail, and he needed a lawyer."

"But why *you*? Why not some other smart-dressed legal beagle?"

"I'm the best, of course."

"How did he know that?"

"My reputation precedes me."

"Why did he have your number on him? He gave your name and number to our operator. I'm curious how he knew that off the top of his head."

Stackler checked his watch again and seemed a bit uncomfortable. "I worked with him before, several years ago. Is this really necessary? I have places to be."

"Several years ago, huh? How did he know to call you then, at that time?"

"Sheriff, you know I don't have to answer that. It's in the past, and has nothing to do with your trumped-up charges against him today. If you don't mind, I'm going to go now. It's been great to meet you, and…" He looked over at Judge Torres and Willie, eyed them up and down and seemed less than impressed. "And very nice *not* to meet whoever you two are. Now let's not see each other until court, okay? 'Bye."

He turned so sharply that the breeze he created rustled papers on Jake's desk. The man's boots sounded in the hallway, fading as he went away. Jake could only snort at his sheer audacity.

"Well!" Willie chuffed. "He's not very nice at all."

"I told you I didn't like his type," Judge Torres said. "But he's definitely hiding something, the way he refused to talk about why he's representing someone like Mason Bannet."

"What do you suppose Mason needed him for several years ago?" Willie asked. "Could it have something to do with the same trouble my stepfather was in?"

"Oh, it won't be too hard to find out," Judge Torres

said. "It's all there, public record, just waiting to be looked up, now that we know what to look for."

Jake was going to get back on his computer, but then he paused. "I think I'd like to talk to Mason first, though. It might be worthwhile to ask him the same questions and see what answers he gives."

"He might not talk to you," the judge noted. "His lawyer just left—he doesn't have to say anything without counsel present."

"Then I'll come back up here and get online."

"Better yet," the judge suggested, "you go talk to him and Willie and I will go online. You can reach us over at our office if you learn anything. Okay with you, Willie?"

"Of course," she said. "Now that we know Mason and Mosey are the same person, I'm eager to see what we can find about him."

Jake gave her an encouraging smile. It was good to see her hopeful again. He was glad the judge had stopped by. No one understood Willie quite like the judge did— he knew what she needed right now was a job. If there was information out there tying Mason to Roy Henner, Willie would find it. And that might just lead them to a killer.

# Chapter Sixteen

Willie scrolled through information on her computer. It felt strange to come back to the office after being so fully immersed in the investigation these last three days. She hardly ever went that long without coming in to work. Perhaps that might be something she needed to rethink, if she was serious about wanting to be more involved with her family.

Judge Torres had gone into his office and was also searching for whatever he could find about past legal run-ins for Mason Bannet. So far Willie hadn't come across anything, but maybe he was doing better. Hopefully Jake would get more information from him in person, though she had to admit that seemed overly optimistic. Mason was not likely to cooperate, and his uptight lawyer had probably instructed him to keep quiet.

She had to give Jake credit for trying, though. Not many men would be so eager to put aside their personal feelings and face the person who had caused so much harm. Jake would do it, though. He'd be calm, controlled and professional. It was simply who he was; Jake would always do the right thing.

Just like he did all those years ago when he notified Children's Services to step in and save her family. Willie had struggled to convince herself they were fine, that she had everything under control then, but she could no longer deny the truth. What Jake did had been a blessing. As a teenager, when Willie prayed for God to take care of her family, He had been working to bring Jake into the picture. He'd been the instrument God used to get her family the help they needed.

And she'd hated him for it.

Well, not anymore. The next time she saw Jake, she'd have to tell him she'd been so very wrong about him for so long. And she'd have to apologize. That wouldn't be easy for her, but Jake deserved it.

Judge Torres suddenly called out, interrupting her thoughts. "Willie! I found something!"

She hurried into his office. He was grinning at her from behind his big cherrywood desk. She took that as a good sign.

"I found his alias, Mosey," the judge said. "There was a sting operation in Dallas, and it ended up snagging your stepfather and several other criminals involved in drug smuggling and burglaries."

"So he did get arrested at the same time Garret did."

"No. His name was mentioned when some of the guys were questioned—including your stepfather—but he was never caught."

"Just like Garret said," she mused. "Do you suppose someone tipped Mason off? Maybe he knew about the sting."

"Could be. But here's the interesting part. One law firm represented several of the guys who got picked up."

"Let me guess—Stackler."

The judge nodded. "Yep. He was a junior partner in a large Dallas firm then, but he definitely worked on at least one of the cases. My guess is the big boss brought in counsel for some petty crook in exchange for the crook keeping the boss's name out of things."

"Makes sense. Just how dirty is this Stackler?"

Judge Torres was leaning in, reading something closely on his screen. "Here's his name in a news article from that time. It's about discrepancies in the law firm—money went missing from some accounts there."

"He was stealing from his own firm?" Willie moved around the desk to see for herself. The judge pointed to the paragraph in question and she read aloud. *"'Spokesman for the firm, Dale Stackler, says, "These accounts involve several clients, but we've found a common link. In each case, one of our junior members was assigned to the accounts, Pamela Laughlin. We're not sure what Ms. Laughlin's involvement has been, but we are looking for her to ask some questions and..."'"*

Willie stopped reading as realization struck her.

"What is it?" the judge asked.

"It's her! It's my Aunt Pam," Willie said, hardly believing it herself. "Laughlin was Aunt Pam's maiden name! And she was a lawyer when she married my uncle."

The judge was already typing another search into his computer. "I remember. She came to work here for a local firm right around that time. It looks like there were never any charges pressed against her, and I don't see other articles about those accusations at all. But look, here's an announcement that Mr. Stackler had left that firm and was hanging out his own shingle...in a very exclusive part of Dallas, I might add. I wonder where he suddenly got the capital for that?"

"Good question," Willie said. "And I wonder why he and Aunt Pam stayed so close all these years, after he went on record accusing her of embezzlement from their old firm."

"That is interesting, isn't it? Let's follow the time-line."

Willie perched on the side of his desk as he tracked back various references and highlights in the timeline. They learned that Pam left the Dallas firm shortly after the sting operation that brought in Garret and some of his cronies. Mason was never implicated, but clearly Stackler was involved in some of the related cases. He could easily have been protecting the bosses at that time. Perhaps if Mason had sensitive information, he had been protected as well. That explained why Mason would have Stackler's phone number close at hand.

Was Aunt Pam really involved in embezzlement at that same time? There was no way to know, but the fact that she left the firm without fanfare, only to resurface a few weeks later here in Laurel County, taking a low-level position in a very small firm, seemed significant. It would be easy to think she was trying to hide from something.

Judge Torres pointed out an additional curious co-incidence. "She came to work for Jimenez and Hays. You know that firm, Willie. Mr. Hays was your grand-father's attorney for many years."

"You're right! But…then Aunt Pam married my uncle, Grandpa died and Roy hired Stackler to handle the estate."

"Well, now that doesn't sound fishy, does it?" The judge chuckled.

"You don't think they had anything shady going on,

do you? Maybe they felt more comfortable working with someone Pam was familiar with. And didn't Mr. Hays retire around then?"

"Before he retired, Hays came and talked to me, asking advice. He didn't tell me who his client was, but it's a small world around here. I didn't have to think too hard to figure out who he was talking about. I didn't know you then, of course, but I knew your grandfather. Hays was working on making the man's will with him."

"You advised him on my grandfather's will?"

"No, he told me his client wanted to leave his ranch to just one heir, not have it divided up. Hays was asking me what I'd do about something like that, how I'd have it drawn up."

"So you suggested the testamentary trust."

"Yes, but the heir he was talking about wasn't Roy, it was you, Willie. I didn't think more of it until years later when you came to work for me. The will Hays was drawing up was *not* the will that ended up on record."

"So why didn't you question it when you first realized it was different?" Jake asked.

"There was no reason to," the judge said with a sigh. "I assumed Vern Henner changed his mind at some point. But now...there are just too many red flags. Do you see here? When Mr. Hays went on medical leave, your aunt took over his accounts, Willie. She would've been the one to finish drawing up your grandfather's will."

"That had to be right around the time she married my uncle. They must've met while she was my grandfather's attorney. But...if she was already the family's attorney, why would my uncle hire Stackler, too?"

"It could be they wanted to avoid the appearance

of anything unethical since your aunt and uncle were married, or..."

"Or maybe they didn't want anyone from Jimenez and Hays to know what they were doing," Willie suggested, trying to keep her voice calm and her anger at bay. "If it's true that my grandfather's original intent was different from what was eventually filed, maybe my aunt and uncle hired Stackler to make sure no one realized the will that went to probate wasn't the will my grandfather drew up. Maybe she falsified the will."

"That's quite an accusation, but it certainly would've been easier to get away with it if the original firm had nothing to do with the probate case. Yes, I can see that. But could they have duped your grandfather? He would've had to sign the will before filing it."

"Oh, come on, you knew my grandfather. He wanted to be outside, on the range or training his horses. He didn't have time to read over legal documents. They could've put something in front of him and told him it was the will he'd been working on with Mr. Hays, and he would have signed. He trusted my uncle."

Judge Torres seemed to consider this, then agreed. "Yes, that sounds like your grandfather. It certainly would explain why Roy has continued to work with Stackler. He's in on the scheme. As long as no one contested the will, who would ever know?"

"What if my mother knew?" Willie said slowly. "She always said she didn't trust that will, that Grandpa would never have left me out of the ranch that way."

Now Judge Torres turned to Willie. His dark eyes flashed under graying eyebrows. "If your mother had any sort of proof to back up her suspicions, that sure might have given someone a motive to get rid of her."

\* \* \*

Jake sat across from Mason, who was behind bars in the holding area. It would be a battle of brains rather than brawn, Jake could tell. If he hoped to get anything useful out of Mason, he was going to have to be smart.

"I'm glad your lawyer was able to get right over here to talk to you," Jake said. "He seems to take an interest in your welfare."

"Yeah, and he told me I don't have to talk to you."

"You don't, not without counsel. But I'm not going to ask you anything about your reasons for being locked up here today."

"Then what's the point?"

"The point is I'm impressed. You've got a big-city lawyer at the top of your contacts list. You call, and he jumps into action."

"You said it yourself—he's interested in my welfare."

"Seems like everyone should have a lawyer like that. Is he taking new clients?"

Mason blatantly laughed at him. "Oh, that's rich! I'd love to see Dale Stackler representing you!"

"Why not? Are you saying I'm not much like his usual clientele?"

"Oh, no, you're not getting me to go there," Mason said. "I'm not talking about the people he represents."

"But you know who they are."

"Maybe I do."

"It doesn't matter. Court documents are public record. I can look them up."

"Then why did you ask about it?"

"I thought you might want to tell me, you know, since you're being so cooperative and all."

"I'm not telling you anything! If you want to talk to me, you can get my lawyer back in here."

"So he would know how to advise you, even if I want to talk about things that happened, oh, twelve years ago? Did you know him back then?"

"You think you're so slick, big sheriff with his big badge. Is that what this is? You brought me in here for taking a swipe at you today, but what you really want is to nail me for making that woman disappear?"

"Did you have anything to do with that?"

"No!"

"Is that the truth, or are you saying what your lawyer told you to say?"

"Of course, it's the truth. I don't need Stackler to tell me what to say about that. I didn't have anything to do with whatever happened to her, and that's just the way it is."

"I want to believe you, Mason."

"I don't care what you believe. I didn't do anything to her."

"That's not what my witness says."

"I argued with her, yeah, but that's all. She got mad, so I left."

"What were you arguing about?"

"None of your business."

"But she ended up dead, Mason. Everything she did during those last few days is my business."

"Is that so? Well, then maybe you ought to go talk to her boyfriend. She was going to see *him* that night."

The information slammed into Jake. He tried not to react. Now that he had Mason talking, the last thing he wanted was to give some cue that might shut him up.

"Don't change the subject. If there was a boyfriend, we would've found him."

"There *was* a boyfriend."

"Who was he?" Jake asked.

"I don't know. All she said was that if I didn't back off and leave her alone, she'd get her boyfriend after me. Said he's a *lawyer*. Like I'm supposed to be afraid of that."

"What lawyer?"

"I don't know. How about you don't expect me to do your job for you? All I know is what she said, then I never saw her again. And that *is* the truth."

"Okay, say I believe you. What made her threaten to get the boyfriend after you? What did you do to her?"

"Nothing! We argued. That's all."

"About what?"

Mason tapped his fingers on the wall beside him and stared at the ceiling. Jake waited. The sounds from the building grew louder around them: doors creaking, the elevator stopping between floors, muffled voices, the ventilation system. Jake didn't budge.

Finally Mason did. "It was about a phone call. I overheard a phone call about Garret."

"He was in prison at that time."

"Yeah, but he left something behind. I was trying to find it."

"What were you trying to find?"

"He stole something, okay? Something my bosses wanted back. I heard Kim on the phone talking about it."

"The drugs?" Jake asked.

"You know about that?"

"I know about a lot of things. Garret says he didn't take that shipment of drugs."

"That's what he told me, but Kim said otherwise."

"She told you about the drugs?"

"No, I overheard her on a phone call."

"Who was she talking to?"

"I don't know. I was hanging out behind the place where she worked, keeping an eye on her, just in case. When she came outside to make a call, I listened in."

"You're a true gentleman, Mason."

"You want me to tell you, or not? She was being really vague...mysterious. She said Garret confessed he knew about this *thing* that was hidden. It made her pretty mad, actually. She says she should have known about it all along, that she knew exactly who to take it to and get what she was owed."

"And you think she was talking about the drugs."

"What else? Garret took them, then finally told her where he hid them. That's what we were arguing about. She tried to deny it all, but I knew."

Jake eyed him, trying to read his motives. "Why are you telling me this?"

"Because I want you to find out who killed that woman! It wasn't me, and I don't want to take the fall for it. You might hate me, Jake, but you are not going to pin murder on me."

Jake met his wild gaze evenly. For the first time since he'd known the man, the walls seemed to come down between them. Jake could see the lost, frightened person that Mason was.

"I don't hate you, Mason," he said quietly. "I'm just sad for you. My sister loved you, unconditionally. That little girl you two have is the most beautiful, tender soul, and she loves you, too. You're so broken that you can't even see it, that you're willing to throw it all away."

As usual, Mason reacted the only way he knew how. With anger.

"Shut up! What do you know about anything in my life? Get out of here, Jake. I'm done talking to you!"

The deputy assigned to the holding area appeared as Mason's voice rose. Jake gave him a nod, and he unlocked the outer room, where Jake was. Mason was still secure in the cell, though he was eyeing Jake furiously.

"Everything okay in there?" the deputy asked.

"Just having a heart-to-heart," Jake replied.

Mason swore under his breath.

The deputy let Jake out and locked the door safely behind him. It was tragic what Mason had done with his life; he could have had so much more happiness. Jake shook off the harsh words and the anger Mason had hurled at him. He'd given solid, useful information, and Jake would focus on that.

How much of it could be trusted, though? It conflicted with Garret's story, though Jake had no reason to trust Garret, either. And what about Mason's claim that Kim did, indeed, have a boyfriend? Jake supposed that could be true, but who would that have been? There'd been no reference to lawyers in her social circle.

Jake paused in the hallway as he signed the log at the intake desk. Stackler was a lawyer. Kim might have met him through Roy and Pam. Could *he* have been involved with her? It didn't seem likely that she would be interested in someone like him, but then again…maybe he'd been interested in her. Maybe Stackler heard the same rumors of stolen drugs that Mason had heard.

Maybe Stackler had been involved with Kim because he was looking for those drugs, too.

Maybe Jake should have asked Stackler a few more questions.

Grabbing his radio, Jake quickly paged the officer on duty at the main entrance. She confirmed that Stackler had left the building some time ago. Jake grumbled to himself.

"You want to talk to that Stackler guy?" the intake officer asked, overhearing Jake on his radio.

"I thought of a few questions I should've asked him before he left."

"Well," the officer replied, "he can't be going too far. I heard him on his cell phone before he left, calling someone to say he'd meet them in fifteen minutes."

"Fifteen minutes? He certainly isn't heading straight back to Dallas, then."

"No, sir. Whoever he's meeting is here in Laurel County. I guess all you have to do is figure out who that is, then you can find him again."

Jake agreed. But how was he going to do that? He didn't know enough about Stackler to be certain whom he might be in contact with here locally. Jake's first instinct was to find Willie. Maybe she could help him figure it out.

Before he could leave the intake area, though, a call came through his radio. It was Dispatch; they thought he'd want to know a report just came in of a disturbance—at Juniper Ridge Ranch.

# *Chapter Seventeen*

"I hope I don't regret this," Jake said.

Willie was sitting beside him in his cruiser as they drove—lights on—toward the ranch. It wasn't his first choice to bring her along, but she insisted that before he rushed over in the middle of a "disturbance," he needed to know what she and the judge had just learned.

"I'll stay in the car once we get there," she assured him. "But you need to know some stuff first."

"I'm all ears. You confirmed Stackler represented some of the people involved in the same criminal activities Mason and Garret were involved in?"

"Yes, we're pretty sure he represented those crime bosses my stepfather worked for. It looks like they hired Stackler to make sure Mason never went to court or testified about anything."

"Because Mason knows a lot more than he's let on, right? I'm not surprised."

"But here's the big thing—it's my Aunt Pam," Willie went on, feeling like she was racing the clock to convey all the necessary information. "She was also an attorney."

"Yes, I remember that. Mason mentioned it, too."

"He probably knows her from back then. She worked for the same legal firm Stackler did. In fact, my aunt left there after being accused of embezzling! Stackler knew about that, too. At first it seemed like he was on the firm's side, against my aunt, but then Pam must have paid him off. The whole embezzlement thing is dropped and suddenly he starts up his own fancy law firm. Next thing you know, he works for the bad guys... and my Uncle Roy."

"Wow."

"But there's more!" she exclaimed.

Willie explained to him what they'd found about Aunt Pam showing up in Laurel County, working for the local law firm, then being the one involved in finishing her grandfather's new will.

"It's crazy, but it all makes sense," he admitted. "Pam worked for a crooked law firm in Dallas, so she would have known how to run her own scheme here in Laurel County. It even makes sense why she would marry your uncle so soon after taking that local job. Roy was a bachelor with a rich elderly father, his only brother had already passed away and everyone knew there was a new will being drawn up."

"A testamentary trust—she didn't even have to invent that. Mr. Hays had already been talking to people about it. All Pam had to do was flip the beneficiaries. With Mr. Hays out of the picture, who would know?"

"So instead of the ranch going to you, it went to your uncle," Jake said, as the cruiser picked up speed. "Too bad there's no way to prove that—it would probably be a big deal to someone."

"Maybe big enough to commit murder?" Willie asked.

He nodded. "Maybe. But if we're talking about Stackler, why would he care who inherited the ranch?"

"Maybe he doesn't. But he knows the stuff my Aunt Pam did…so maybe he was using that against them."

"Blackmail? That could be. They certainly would have all sorts of reasons to keep everything hushed up. And if your mother found out about any of it…"

"Stackler's gravy train would derail," Willie said, realizing what that might mean. "He would've done almost anything to keep my mother quiet!"

He gave a worried sigh. "And here I am driving you over there, where we expect to find Stackler in the middle of a disturbance. I should *not* have invited you along."

"Too late now."

"You *will* stay in the car," he insisted.

"I already agreed to that."

"Something tells me I need to remind you."

She scowled at him but wasn't honestly upset. It was kind of nice that he worried about her. Besides, they didn't know what they were getting into. Dispatch hadn't been able to give any other details—the phone disconnected after the caller requested assistance. All they knew was something was happening at the ranch, and there was a strong likelihood that Dale Stackler was involved. Given what they knew of his past, he could be capable of anything.

The two cruisers in front of Jake left clouds of dust as they pulled off the main road and through the gates of Juniper Ridge Ranch. Willie noted that they didn't appear to slow down very much, so she braced herself for a rough ride as Jake whipped his car close behind.

They bounced along until the homestead came into

view, the buildings clustered together appearing like looming shadows through the dusty haze in the air. Willie could see several vehicles already parked near the house. One older pickup parked there caught her eye.

"That truck—the red one—I think I recognize it," she said as Jake skidded to a stop.

"Your uncle's?"

"No, I'm pretty sure we saw it at the Hickman Ranch. I think it might be Garret's!"

Jake didn't reply, but quickly grabbed for his radio, advising his deputies that there could be multiple people on site. They didn't actually see anyone, though, so Willie could only wonder what they'd encounter. Jake unfastened his seat belt and turned to her.

"I'll go up to the house," he said, meeting her gaze with an intensity she knew not to disregard. "Stay here and stay safe."

"Do you want me to do anything, or call anybody for backup?"

He opened the door to climb out. "You could say a prayer."

"I will. Just…be careful, Jake."

"That's what I do," he said, sparing one priceless moment to give her a reassuring smile. Then he was out of the car.

Willie listened through the half-open window. Jake met his deputies and barked instructions. Willie held her breath and watched Jake head toward the wide porch that wrapped two sides of the house. It seemed the perfect time to make good on her promise to say that prayer.

*Lord, please go with Jake. Be by his side, guide his words and give him wisdom for whatever situation he*

*finds. Let Your spirit flow through everyone involved
so they don't give in to anger or violence. Cover us
with grace, dear Heavenly Father. We need it so badly
right now.*

Jake had not quite made it to the front door when it
opened peacefully. Willie watched intently, craning her
neck for a better view. Aunt Pam stepped out to greet
Jake there. Willie let out a sigh of relief; Pam didn't
seem flustered or frightened or harmed in any way.
Perhaps the reports of a disturbance were unfounded.

But then Pam was pointing off in another direction.
Willie could see that she gestured toward the old bunkhouse. No, not toward the bunkhouse…behind it. Where
that old shed sat, just out of view from here. Jake motioned for his deputies to follow and immediately took
off in that direction.

Willie ached to go with him. What was happening?
Could that familiar truck parked nearby truly belong to
her stepfather? A sleek silver sedan was also parked in
front of the house, and Willie assumed it must belong
to Dale Stackler. Was Uncle Roy out in the shed with
the scheming lawyer and Garret Landers? What were
they searching for?

There was no way for Willie to know. Jake and his
deputies were quickly gone, out of view behind the bunkhouse. She listened carefully, but other than the distant
murmur of voices, she heard nothing to give her any idea
what was transpiring. Was Jake in danger? She clenched
her hands and sent up a fervent prayer.

"Willie?" Her aunt had noticed her and called out.

Willie glanced toward the house. Aunt Pam was leaving the porch and coming her way. Willie took that as
a good sign, that Pam felt secure enough to leave the

safety of her home. But the sour expression on Pam's face indicated that even though there might not be imminent violence, she wasn't overly pleased to have company.

"So you're responding to calls with the sheriff now?" Pam said as she approached.

"It was convenient," Willie replied simply. "But what's going on here? Is that Garret's truck?"

Pam nodded. "How did you know that?"

"And what about Dale Stackler?" Willie asked, ignoring the question. "Is he here, too?"

Pam seemed surprised she'd know that as well. "Yes, they all went out to the old tool shed."

"What are they doing out there?"

"I told you, Roy wants to get rid of the tools and tear it down."

"But there's been an order not to interfere with the investigation, not to remove things from the site."

"Well, I guess Garret didn't get the memo on that. He was already scheduled to come out here and pick up his stuff."

"*His* stuff?"

"He's the one who called Roy a few days ago asking about it," Pam explained with a frustrated sigh. "Apparently he left some things in it years ago when he was still working here on the ranch."

"You didn't say it was his stuff in there, you said he wanted Roy's old tools."

"Oh, well, he wants some of those, too," Pam said.

Willie wondered if it could be that simple, or if there was more to it. Had Garret arranged to get those tools before or after she found her mother's body? The timing on this would certainly be an important piece of the puzzle. But who had called the sheriff's office about it?

She didn't get to ask her aunt about that, though. They were interrupted by bellowing from near the bunkhouse. Uncle Roy appeared, heading their way, and he didn't seem any too happy.

"Why'd you call the cops, Pam?" he called to his wife. "We don't need the sheriff out here!"

"I didn't call anyone," Pam insisted. "I don't know who did."

Roy scowled at her, then his eyes fell on Willie as he crunched toward the assortment of vehicles parked near the house. He snarled at his niece.

"What are you doing here? Did *you* call the cops?"

"Me? Why would I call them?" she replied through the open window. "I have no idea what's been going on out here."

Just then Garret and Stackler appeared, flanked by Jake and his deputies. Thankfully, everyone seemed calm, and Willie was pleased to see no weapons were drawn. Aside from Roy's usual bad attitude, there was no indication of trouble.

Aunt Pam, on the other hand, eyed Willie suspiciously. "You knew Garret was here. And somehow you knew our attorney was, too. What are you trying to do, Willie? Did you think you could catch us in some kind of conspiracy?"

Willie was caught off guard by the accusation.

"I don't know, Aunt Pam," she snapped loudly enough so everyone could hear. "Is that what this is, some kind of conspiracy?"

"Don't get smart with me," Uncle Roy said, apparently forgetting she was an adult and no longer an unwanted child in his home. "It's bad enough that you've obviously been telling stories to your new friend the sheriff, but calling him out here on some bogus report? That's a criminal offense, Willie."

"She didn't call us," Jake said, stepping between Roy and the cruiser. "Now, if everyone would settle down, maybe we can figure out what's going on."

"There's nothing going on. That's what I keep telling you," Roy said.

But Jake wasn't backing down. "Obviously something is going on. You were rummaging in that shed with these two, and I'm pretty sure there's still a court order telling you to stay *out* of there."

"You already sent your team to go through there," Roy said. "They didn't find anything, did they? There's no reason at all I shouldn't be allowed back into my own shed now."

"There *is* a reason," Jake said firmly. "A woman's body was found on your property—a woman who was murdered! So far we haven't found the murder weapon or determined exactly where the murder took place. That gives us more than enough reason to tell you to wait until we have conducted all our searches before you enter areas in question."

"Well, that doesn't give Willie the right to go calling in reports for you to come rushing out here," Roy grumbled.

Finally someone else spoke up. It was Garret. "She didn't call. I did."

"You did?" Jake asked.

Willie was as surprised as everyone else seemed to be. All eyes turned to her former stepfather. Garret cleared his voice then explained.

"I didn't know that shed was off-limits until I got here," he said. "I was coming by to pick up a box of things that got left here when I quit. Roy mentioned he had some old tools to get rid of, so I thought I might buy some of them cheap while I was here. You can never have too many tools, you know."

"When did you arrange all this?" Jake asked.

"A couple days ago!" Pam said quickly. "Isn't that what you said, Roy? Garret called you a couple days ago? Just after we heard about finding Kim's body, I think."

Roy frowned, then quickly agreed with his wife. "Yeah."

Jake looked to Garret. "Is that true? You called Roy two days ago?"

Garret shook his head. "Not quite. He did call me yesterday, but we'd already talked about the tools. That was a couple weeks ago, when he came by the ranch to talk to my boss, Mr. Hickman."

Jake looked back at Roy. "Why did you go see Mr. Hickman?"

"About business."

"What kind of business?" Jake persisted.

"None of yours! It didn't have anything to do with murder or secret weapons or anything."

"My client went to speak with Mr. Hickman regarding the sale of this ranch," Stackler chimed in, suddenly becoming helpful. Roy shot him a warning look, but the attorney brushed it off with a brief explanation. "We might as well tell him, Roy. You've got nothing to hide. Yes, Sheriff, he went to talk to Mr. Hickman about the possibility of selling this ranch to him. Apparently, he saw Garret while he was there and mentioned he was

getting ready to clean out the shed and wanted to un-
load some old tools. It's as simple as that. Perfectly innocent, and it all happened before anyone even knew
there was a crime scene."

"So Mr. Hickman is buying the ranch?" Willie asked.

"No," Roy said. "He declined, but someone else
turned up a few days later interested in buying. I didn't
want to lose him, so I thought I'd try to make the place
look as good as possible. Pam's been after me for ages
to tear that old shed down and burn it, so you see? That's
why I wanted to work on that, why I called Garret yesterday to come get his things."

"What about the box?" Jake asked, gesturing toward
a box that one of the deputies had tucked under his arm.
"If it was a simple matter of Garret coming over to pick
up some old tools, why do you have this old box addressed to him?"

"I told you, I don't know anything about that," Roy
said. "If it's so important, why didn't your deputies find
that when they searched the place?"

Jake ignored him and turned to Garret. "What's in
the box?"

Garret shrugged. "I don't know. I don't remember
that box. I found it in there, hidden pretty good."

"Why don't we just open it?" Roy grumbled.

"Are you sure you want him to do that?" Stackler
cautioned. "He's not waving a search warrant in your
face. You don't have to let him."

"It doesn't matter to me," Roy insisted. "That's not
my name on the box. I didn't put anything incriminat-
ing in there."

"Listen to the lawyer, Roy," Pam said. "The sheriff
doesn't have a right to go through our things—"

"But I do," Jake reminded them. "A search warrant was issued—it specifically mentions that shed and the contents to be searched and any probable weapon to be retrieved."

"You think there's a murder weapon in that box?" Pam asked skeptically.

"I'll have my client drag you to court if you so much as try to open that box," Stackler said. "This is clearly overreach and harassment."

"But that isn't my box!" Roy insisted. "If there's any sort of weapon inside, it isn't mine."

"It's mine," Garret declared. "It's got my name on it, right? So go ahead and open it, Sheriff. Let's find out what's in there."

Jake motioned for the deputy to set the box on the trunk of the car. Willie quickly jumped out and joined the group at the rear of the cruiser. Pulling out his knife, Jake started cutting the tape that sealed the box shut. Willie pushed up close to her aunt and leaned in to watch.

Her gaze caught on the name written carefully on the box. Willie gasped.

"That's my mother's writing!" she cried.

Jake paused. Garret leaned over and peered at the box.

"She's right," he agreed. "That's Kim's handwriting. See how she put that little extra loop in the *G* at the front of my name? Yeah, I recognize that. It sure takes me back."

"Well, she did live here at one point," Pam said sharply. "She probably boxed this up for you when you were moving out and somehow it didn't get put on the truck."

"Maybe." Garret sighed. "It sure is like a blast from the past, seeing my name the way she used to write it. Go ahead, Sheriff. Open the box."

Jake glanced around. Willie could feel the anticipation growing. Her aunt shifted nervously, Uncle Roy cleared his throat and Dale Stackler rolled his eyes as if he was bored with the whole thing.

Willie held her breath as Jake pulled up the flaps on the box to reveal what was inside.

# Chapter Eighteen

Jake pried the box gingerly. It had clearly been stored in that shed for a while. The cardboard was brittle, and he didn't want to risk damaging whatever was inside. He knew the suspense must be terrible for Willie, but he took his time.

Once inside the box, several crumpled sheets of newspaper had to be removed. He pulled them away carefully. One of his deputies remarked on the date printed at the top of a page.

"It's from twelve years ago!"

This revelation made Jake's task all the more important. He continued slowly, removing the packing material until he found an envelope, also addressed to Garret. Below that was a package of some sort. Jake handed the envelope to his deputy then gently reached for the package. He pulled it out—very quickly, the contents were evident.

"It's socks!" Roy exclaimed.

Everyone was silent for a second, then suddenly Garret threw back his head and laughed.

"She was sending me socks! Well, bless her. I thought

that dear woman hated me after all I did…but she was sending me socks."

"You mean…you think this box was supposed to go to you in prison?" Willie asked.

"By the date on those newspapers, yes," Garret said. "I can't believe it…she was sending me socks. After all that time when I finally wrote to her, I never heard back. I thought she didn't want to talk to me again, and who could blame her? But look at that, she was getting ready to send me some socks."

"Here, this letter is for you," Jake said as his deputy gave Garret the envelope.

"This is ridiculous!" Pam said. "It's obvious this box of socks doesn't have anything to do with us. I think you all should leave—take your things and go."

"No, I think we'll stay a little while longer," Jake said, watching as Garret unfolded a letter that he had never hoped to see.

Willie was, understandably, interested, too. Her bright eyes were glued on Garret, taking in his expression as he scanned the letter. As if he understood her interest, he read aloud.

"'Garret, I can't say I'm surprised to hear you got yourself locked up, but I'm happy you're finally safe. It was tough when you left and I was angry, but most of all I worried for you. I prayed you'd find your way eventually and I'm glad your letter tells me you're on a better path now. What a blessing.

"'Thank you for reaching out and for thinking of Willie now that her grandpa is gone. She misses him every day. You mentioned what you heard about her inheritance. Sadly, it's true. It's not what we expected, but when she is eighteen she'll have money for college.

*Vern always told me he planned to leave the ranch to
Willie, so this surprised us, but we trusted Roy.*

"'I don't anymore. Part of my job at the print shop
is shredding documents for businesses. In a box of old
files from a law firm, I found draft copies of Vern's
original will! They give the ranch in trust to my Willie,
just like Vern said he would do.*

"'I didn't shred those. Is this proof that Roy inten-
tionally cheated Willie? Hard to believe, but from what
you say about that hidden thing you found, I guess it's
not so far-fetched. Roy's lawyer might know something,
so I sort of made friends with him. He might tell me
something, so I'll let you know.*

"'For now, I hope the socks make your life a little
better. I don't know if you get care packs from anyone,
but I read that prisoners need t-shirts and socks. Next
month I'll send you t-shirts. God bless you, Garret.
Take care.'"*

Garret dabbed the corners of his eyes. Jake felt a
lump in his own throat as the man read that heartfelt
letter from so long ago. No wonder Willie turned out to
be such an amazing person. Even after everything Kim
Milson had been through, she still had compassion for
her ex-husband in prison. Even through her own pain,
she worried for his safety...and his soul.

"She dated the letter," Garret added. "When did you
say she disappeared?"

Jake glanced at the letter. He almost wished Willie
hadn't seen it, but he knew she had. She drew a sharp
breath and put her hand to her lips.

"That's two days before she disappeared," Jake answered. "That's probably why you never got that package. She put your name on it, but she must have needed

to look up the prison address before she could add it to the package. Whatever happened to her...that never got mailed."

Which begged the obvious question.

"Then how did it end up in Uncle Roy's shed?" Willie demanded.

Roy was already taking a step back, waving his hands in denial. "Oh, no, I have nothing to do with this! I've never seen that box before."

"It was in your shed, Roy," Jake pointed out.

"Maybe don't say anything more," Stackler advised his client.

But Roy was adamant. "I don't have anything more to say! I know nothing about that box. I haven't even been in that shed in... I don't know how long. It's a hazard. Pam said last time she was out there the floor nearly fell in and she saw rattlesnakes nesting underneath."

"So Pam has been in the shed?" Jake asked.

"I have not!" Pam declared, then turned to the attorney. "Do something, make him stop talking."

"I can't make him stop talking," Stackler replied. "If he wants to hang himself..."

"I am not hanging myself!" Roy nearly shouted. "You two keep acting like you think I'm guilty of something, but I'm not!"

Then Roy turned to Jake. His eyes were wild, and he seemed on the verge of panic. He pointed frantically at Stackler. "It's him! He's the one. He's been covering this up all along. First, it was his idea to redo the will, and—"

"Oh, no, that was not my idea," Stacker interrupted. "That was all your doing, Roy. Pam contacted me and told me you were forcing her to fix that will or you would refuse to marry her."

"What? I never told her to fix anything! She told me the will was a mess, that the old guy who was working on it was getting ready to retire, and he'd been too sick to work on it so she had to take over. She's the one who finished drawing it up for my father—she did it while he was still alive, and he signed it."

"Did he, though?" Jake asked. "You didn't maybe fudge that signature?"

"No! Of course not. Pam got the will ready, and I took it in and had him sign it."

Jake was beginning to sense that Willie's suspicions were well-founded. He'd been watching her eyes go round as the others had been arguing. Jake nodded to his deputies, warning them to be on their guard. Things might get dicey.

"Did your father read that will carefully before he signed it, Roy?"

"Why should he read it?" Roy asked. "He was the one who wrote it."

"Maybe what he wrote were those draft copies my mother pulled from the shred pile!" Willie said. "He probably thought that was the will he was signing."

Jake turned to Pam. "Did you change the will to favor Roy?"

Pam sputtered an unintelligible answer. Roy glared at her as if seeing her for the first time. If his shock wasn't genuine, he certainly was a good actor.

"Is—is that what you did, Pam?" he stammered. "You told me my father wanted *me* to have the ranch once he saw that I was getting married. Was that a lie?"

Pam simply rolled her eyes at this. "He knew you

never had a clue how to run this place—you ran it right into the ground."

"Well, you were no help," Roy countered. "Anytime I wanted to do something, you said I had to clear it through our lawyer. He never approved anything!"

"It's his job to keep you from messing up, Roy."

Jake watched Willie as she was audience to this dysfunction. He could see the pain at being betrayed on her face. It was obvious she'd been cheated by the very people who were supposed to have her interests at heart. And one of these people may have murdered her mother.

Roy unloaded an angry tirade. "What's your real role in this, Dale? I wanted to expand the range, open up more area for a bigger herd, but you insisted I leave things the way they were. I wanted to work on the water flow, to reroute the creek for better irrigation, but you wouldn't let me touch the creek beds. That's where Kim's body was found! You knew she was out there, didn't you?"

The nervous attorney tried to back away, but the deputies quickly held him. He vehemently hurled accusations right back at Roy.

"I didn't know half as much as you did! Pam told me what happened. I spent the last twelve years covering for what you did to that woman."

"What *I* did?" Roy squawked. "I didn't do anything to her. I thought she left! Garret dumped her, she had all those kids…it just made sense that she took off. You're the one who had a reason to get rid of her. That letter he read…it says she befriended you. Maybe you thought she was asking too many questions."

Pam joined her husband in blaming their lawyer.

"It's true, Dale. You were dating her to find those missing drugs! Maybe you found them then got rid of her."

"Don't point fingers at me! You were the one who got upset when I told you she knew about the will," Stackler snarled. "You orchestrated that switch, Pam. I won't deny it anymore. How stupid were you, to leave old draft copies of the real will in that other lawyer's office?"

"Fine! I'll admit I changed the will, all right? Vern Henner drafted a will that put the ranch in trust for Willie and left some sad little lump sum for Roy. I helped him write it. When it came time to file the will, though, I realized how easy it would be to switch the names around. Vern already read it so many times—he signed without noticing. Once he passed away, Roy hired Dale. He wasn't going to question the will, was he?"

"My mother questioned it," Willie pointed out.

Jake's muscles tensed. He was ready to jump in should anyone resort to violence now that the truth was coming out. But no one moved. Willie maintained her composure, meeting Pam's gaze with bold determination. As painful as this must have been, she obviously wasn't backing down.

Pam shifted her focus to Stackler. "Just one more reason you wanted her quiet. It was you—you killed her, Dale!"

The angry attorney stared right back at her. "Did I? And what weapon did I use?"

"How do I know?" Pam hissed. "They'll probably never find it, whatever it was."

"But what if I tell them where to look?"

Pam tried to maintain her cool, confident demeanor,

but Jake saw it cracking. "Well then… I guess that will just prove you're the murderer."

"You didn't think I knew where you hid it, did you?" Stackler asked, his oily smile growing.

"You're making things up!" Pam snapped.

"What is he talking about?" Roy asked. "Pam? What did you do?"

"Nothing!" she insisted. "Sheriff, arrest this man! Dale Stackler killed Kim Milson, and I will testify. He was dating her so she'd give him the drugs. Then she found out he was involved with switching the will, so he killed her and hid her body out on the range somewhere."

Jake would have loved nothing better than to arrest Stackler and wipe that arrogant smirk off his face, but he was quickly becoming convinced that Stackler was the one telling the truth right now. The more panicked Pam became, the more evident her guilt was.

"How do you know all this, Mrs. Henner?" Jake asked.

"He told me! I should have turned him in, but…he's been blackmailing me, Sheriff! I'm sorry, but I've been so afraid of him all these years."

"Give me a break!" Stackler snarled.

Jake ignored him and kept his focus on Pam. "Blackmailing you? How?"

"I stole some money a long time ago from a firm where I used to work. Dale worked there, too, and he knew what I did. So he followed me here to Laurel County, and he's been forcing us to give him money to keep everything quiet. You don't know the sort of person he really is!"

"Oh, I think I have a pretty good idea," Jake said, finally turning to the seething lawyer. "I know about the embezzlement, and we figured that was the hold you had over them, Stackler. How much have you gotten from them over the years? That's the real reason the ranch failed, isn't it? You've drained them dry."

Garret snapped angrily at Roy. "Hey, that's where all the money I sent for my kids went, wasn't it? You used that money to pay off this guy!"

Roy defended himself. "Of course not. That money went straight into our account and Pam sent out a check every month to... Wait. Pam, did you send that money to Willie?"

Pam could only shrug. "He said he'd blab if we didn't keep paying! He took the kids' money *and* he murdered Kim!"

Stackler growled. "I might have taken your money, but you never told me it was for kids. And I didn't murder that woman!" His wild eyes narrowed and his gaze came to fix on Willie's aunt. "She did it. Pam lured Kim out here and killed her."

Willie stared from Stackler to her aunt in stunned silence. *Aunt Pam murdered my mom?* She didn't want to believe it—had no reason to trust Stackler's accusation. But somehow, she couldn't quite discount it, either.

"She did it right over there," Stackler declared. "In her studio."

"Shut up!" Pam ordered.

Uncle Roy was clearly shocked. "You—you *killed* her? All this time I've been draining every penny we had because you said we had to keep him quiet about the embezzlement, but really he's been covering your *murder*?"

"Oh, he has plenty reason to keep quiet about it," Pam sneered. "He's guilty as anything."

Stackler just kept grinning and shook his head. "Not as guilty as you, Pam! You tried to make me think Roy did it. I thought I was covering for *him* all this time… but today I finally figured it all out. It was one-hundred-percent you."

Roy seemed honestly offended. "You made him think *I* did it?"

"You should have done it," Pam grumbled. "This whole thing was about making sure *you* got your father's ranch. *You* should have been the one to shut her up when she came here waving those copies of that will around. *You* should have been the one to drag her out there in the middle of the night and hope the coyotes got to her before someone could find her. *You* should have figured out a way to get rid of Dale so we didn't have to give him everything we ever earned! You should have done all of that, Roy, but you didn't. You just didn't do anything."

Pam sagged, as if she simply had nothing left in her. She showed no remorse for the tragedy she'd caused or acknowledgment of Willie's pain. She didn't even seem to remember that Kim Milson had been a living, breathing human being whose life was so much more than an inconvenience.

Willie realized she'd been holding her breath. Now that it was out in the open, she drew in a long gasp of air. They had all the pieces to this puzzle. Pam's wall of lies had come crashing down when she admitted her guilt. Willie ached as if she'd just lost her mother all over again.

Jake moved closer to Willie, sensing she needed him. "How did you kill her, Pam?"

"As counsel for Ms. Henner," Stackler inserted, "I should probably advise her not to answer any more questions. But since I have a feeling I'm already fired, and in case you get ideas about pegging me as accessory to this murder, Sheriff, I might as well tell what I know."

"Don't say anything!" Roy ordered. "You owe us this, Dale."

"I don't owe you anything! My loyalty is to myself, and I'm not taking the rap. So here it is. Yes, it's true I was supposed to meet Kim the night she disappeared. Pam wanted me to get close to her to find out how much she knew, so I started going out with her."

"My mother wasn't taken in by your sleazy charm," Willie noted. "Her letter says she was going out with you to find out what *you* knew."

"Obviously we were *not* soul mates," Stackler said. "But I told Kim to meet me here and we'd confront Roy and Pam together, and I really thought that's what we'd do. I figured they'd get scared, and maybe they'd pay me a little more to hush it all up, to bury whatever information Kim had."

"But Pam thought she'd rather bury Kim," Jake said.

"Exactly!" Stackler confirmed. "I think she had it all planned out before Kim even showed up—it was premeditated. You should write that down, Sheriff. You can use it later when you charge her."

"Continue with the story, please," Jake said without emotion.

"Fine. I got here first. Pam was there, in her studio working on that art project that was being dedicated at the sheriff's office the next day. You know the one—I saw it there this afternoon."

"We know the piece," Willie said. "What happened next?"

"Roy wasn't around. Pam had sent him off on some errand—to get him out of the way, I guess. I warned Pam that Kim wasn't some brainless waif and she might really know something, but Pam shut me down. Then we saw Kim's headlights turning off the road and coming toward the house. Pam had me pull my car behind the old bunkhouse so Kim wouldn't see it. She told me to wait there, out of sight."

"So you didn't see what happened?" Willie asked.

"Oh, yes, I did!" Stackler insisted. "I didn't wait in my car. I stood in the shadows to watch. Kim was waving papers in Pam's face. It looked like she had some proof. Pam got angry, but then she calmed down. She had Kim pull her car into one of the bays in her studio. They shut the door and I didn't see what happened after that. Next thing I know, another car is coming up the drive. This time it's Roy."

"He got home while you and Kim were both there?"

"Yeah. He starts heading up to the house but sees the light in the studio so he goes in there first. I hear yelling, then nothing. He storms out and goes up to the house. When he's gone, Pam comes out to find me. She says Roy did a bad thing and I have to come help her."

"She blamed Roy?"

"We go into the studio. I don't see Kim until we walk around the car. She's there on the floor with her head cracked open and the bloo— Well, sorry. That's what I saw."

"All right," Jake said. "We can finish this in my office."

"No, I want to hear the rest," Willie declared. "You believed it was Roy who did it, but what made you change your mind?"

Stackler continued. "She told me Roy got mad at Kim and pushed her, she hit her head. But Pam didn't know I saw the murder weapon."

Jake practically jumped into action. "There's a chance we might still find it around here!"

Stackler shook his head. "No, she got it out of here right away. I didn't realize that's what it was until I saw it again today."

"Did you see it out in the shed?" Roy asked. "Is it one of those old tools?"

Stackler merely sneered. "No, it's not out there. The only thing she's been worried about in the shed has been that box you found."

"You knew about the box?" Jake glared at Pam.

"We found it that night," Stackler confirmed. "We put Kim in her car after she was…well, you know. That's when we saw the box with your name on it. Pam told me to take Kim out to the range and dump her, then get rid of the car. But she didn't want to leave the box—we had no idea what was in it, so Pam told me to take it and destroy it."

"You didn't, though," Jake pointed out.

"I didn't have time. I took it into that shed and hid it under a bunch of stuff then told her it was taken care of."

"I never knew any of this!" Roy said.

"You were blind to everything your wife did," Stackler muttered with a frustrated sigh. "But you must have known something, Roy. You kept handing me money."

Roy shook his head sadly. "I was protecting her for the embezzlement. And the will... I guess I didn't want to know the truth. But about the murder... I didn't know. I never saw anything in that studio. That was Pam's sanctuary. I was barely allowed inside the door. As if I could damage one of those big clumsy sculptures she was making back then."

"And the murder weapon?" Jake asked.

"I didn't see it!" Roy insisted. "No body, no crime scene, no weapon—just all the stuff for that sculpture she was so proud of."

Jake turned back to Stackler. "So you removed Kim's body?"

The lawyer smiled, proud to have a secret. "I drove her out to the range where I figured no one would find her. Then I hid her car where I could go back to it later, which I did. It's at the bottom of Lake Buchanan now. But that night, the house was dark when I got back. Roy must have gone to bed, but Pam was cleaning up her studio."

"And the weapon?"

"She hid it in plain sight. You can go look at it right now, Sheriff. It's part of that art display. It's a big, rough iron bar—she welded it right onto the piece."

Willie felt almost dizzy from shock. She and Jake had commented on that very piece earlier today! It was amazing, all these years she'd never noticed, but today her eye caught on it right away. She knew something was off, that one of the elements didn't fit in with the others. Well, now they knew why. Pam really had been in a rush when she welded that part onto the rest.

"It's part of her sculpture?" Roy gasped.

"When she carried it out of her studio the next day,

it went directly into that fancy display in the courthouse, didn't it?" Stackler asked. "She hid it right in plain sight. I guess it's been locked up there ever since. Maybe she didn't even get all the traces of blood off it—might want to check that."

"I believe I will," Jake announced. "All right, let's take this circus downtown. I'm arresting you, Pam Henner, on suspicion of murder. Roy Henner, I'm arresting you for fraud, and Dale Stackler, you're being charged with tampering, obstruction, abuse of a corpse and just about everything else."

"You'll never make it stick!" Stackler taunted. "I know important people!"

Jake shook his head and motioned for his deputies. Willie was happy to stand back and let him work. She never realized finding the truth would be so exhausting.

"You doing okay?" Jake asked, pausing a moment to lay a hand on her shoulder.

She managed a grateful, yet feeble, smile. "Yeah… I could use a nap."

# Chapter Nineteen

Jake stood in the cool night air and stretched his aching limbs. The afternoon had been spent in his office, filling out reports and gathering as much information as he could on the case. His three newest prisoners had seemed only too happy to spill every juicy bit of gossip they could about each other. It was tragic how quickly they'd turned from desperately protecting each others' secrets to vehemently stumbling over themselves to share them.

Jake was glad for a break. He'd called Jessica to check on her and Shaye, only to be reminded that tonight was the festival fireworks display. They'd been invited to join the families of Jessica's students to gather at the fairgrounds to enjoy the display. Jess offered to bring him along, but he declined the invitation. Nothing sounded better right now than kicking his feet up and having some peace and quiet.

There were lights and sounds from the festival area on the square beyond the courthouse, but things were dark and silent here on this side of downtown. Huge oak trees lined the parking area beside the municipal building, and Jake headed that way. As he reached the row of sheriff's vehicles parked there, he noticed one lone truck parked at the far end of the lot.

It was Willie's. Their law office shared this lot. What was she doing, still working so late? He started walking over there.

But the windows in her office were dark. Then he realized her truck wasn't empty. He could see Willie's silhouette in the back, propped up comfortably in the truck bed. The big, furry shape of her dog was right next to her.

"What are you doing out here?" Jake called as he approached.

Timber barked.

"We're watching the fireworks," Willie called back.

Jake glanced up at the sky. "I don't see any."

"They're starting in five minutes."

"Shouldn't you be over at the fairgrounds? Isn't that where they're lighting them?"

"Timber doesn't like to be so close. Besides, I don't think I can take any more crowds today."

"I hear you there," Jake agreed.

"Come on up," Willie invited. "They'll look really nice from here, popping out from behind the courthouse."

Jake was close enough to see her features clearly. She looked truly relaxed there, sitting on some old patio cushions she must've thrown into the truck just for this occasion. Her smile was honest and inviting. How could he turn her down?

"All right," he said, swinging up onto the tailgate. "If Timber doesn't mind me crashing the party."

In response, Timber hurried over to lick his face in

greeting. Willie laughed and offered Jake a cushion. He accepted and made himself comfortable. Moonlight filtered through the oak trees, and stars made a glittering frame around the looming clock tower on the courthouse.

"I have to admit, this is much better than sitting in a lawn chair with the rest of the county over at the fairgrounds." He sighed as he settled in next to her.

"Right? And no traffic to fight when it's over."

"Smart thinking. So how come Abby and Mac aren't with you?"

"They've got friends to hang out with, and that's okay. I caught them up on the basics of the case this afternoon. Honestly, it doesn't seem to be affecting them much. They say they're relieved to finally have answers, but I'm not sure if this has much impact on their lives at all."

"Give it time," Jake advised. "This is all very new information—it'll take a while to really sink in. Just be there for them when they do start to process it on a deeper level."

"You're probably right. They want to plan a memorial for her, but not now. Maybe near Thanksgiving. Maggie's mother even asked if she could help me with that, so I don't have to do all the planning myself."

"Wow, that's really thoughtful. I hope you'll let her. She probably needs a way to express all her emotions, too. After all, if your mother hadn't died, Barb Westerson never would have become Maggie's mother."

"I guess I hadn't thought of it from her perspective. You're right, that's quite a burden for her to carry."

"I can't think of anyone better to help her carry it. You're pretty amazing, Willie Henner. I hope you realize that. Your mother's been missing for twelve years now, and over the course of one week you found her body, tracked down her killer, regained your inheritance and put on one stellar Heritage Festival. Oh, and you made my sister smile like I haven't seen in years. Your compliments of her art show meant more to her than you can imagine."

"I'm glad she's doing so well. I've missed her, Jake. I hope she'll let me be her friend again."

"I think that's a given. As more and more charges pile onto Mason, she might have to testify against him. She'll need a good friend by her."

"I'll be there for her. Will he face drug charges from his past, too?"

"Stackler was happy to sing about Mason's involvement in the drug operation that sent Garret to jail. He knows a lot of things are going to come to light now, so he's hoping his cooperation gives him some immunity."

"What about that missing drug shipment Stackler was after?" she asked. "Do you think my mother really knew anything about that?"

Jake chuckled and shook his head. "No, it turns out there wasn't any missing drug shipment. It was only a rumor."

"But in her letter, she said Garret mentioned something hidden."

"He told her about an old news clipping he found hidden in Roy's desk years ago. It was about Pam's involvement in that embezzlement. When Garret heard Roy inherited instead of you, he realized Kim ought to know Pam was crooked."

"So Stackler and Mason were barking up the wrong tree the whole time?"

Jake confirmed it. "Garret never stole more than a few little bags."

"Now Mason and Stackler are tattling on each other. That seems fitting."

"The courts are going to be busy for a while on all this. I'm even getting a court order to have your aunt's art display tested for residue. Who knows, we might get our smoking gun after all."

"And Garret? Where does he fit in?"

"Everything he told us checks out." Jake watched her eyes, hoping his words offered relief. "He's been clean and honest since he got out of prison. It seems he's a pretty decent guy, in the end. You think you'll keep in touch?"

She sighed. "I don't know. I believe God can redeem lost souls, plus Abby and Mac deserve to have a father, but only if that's what's really best for them. I guess we'll just have to pray about it, see what God has planned."

"I'm sure it'll be clear to you over time."

"That's what I'm praying for," she said, her eyes bright with hope. "You know... I'm glad for all that's happened these last few days. I can honestly say I feel closer to God than I have for a long while."

"Why do you think that is?"

"I suppose because it's the first time I had to step back and admit I wasn't in charge. I couldn't pretend this was something I could control. I had to rely on Him, and I haven't done that for a while."

"It feels good, doesn't it? I don't know why I need so many constant reminders, but I do," he admitted. "I catch myself thinking God relies on me, when really it's me who needs to rely on Him."

"Maybe that's something we can work on together," she said slowly, meeting his eyes. "You know, help each other remember that."

"I'd like that."

She didn't turn away or brush him off, so he let his gaze linger just a little bit longer. The darkness made her eyes seem endlessly deep, and the streetlights around made them glitter and shine. Or maybe that was something inside her shining so brightly. Whichever it was, he couldn't break the silent connection that grew between them.

"I was terrible to you for too many years, Jake," she said in almost a whisper. "I'm so sorry for that. It was all because I didn't want to admit I needed help."

"You wanted to protect your family, and you did an amazing job, Willie," he replied. "I'm sorry you had to resent me for what I did, but I'd like to think that's all in the past."

"It is, if you can forgive me."

"Of course, I forgive you!" The breeze picked up and he brushed a wayward strand of hair away from her cheek. "Just don't ask me to forget you."

"I hope you never do that, Jake."

He waited for her to add something, to make a teasing remark to keep things casual and light between them. But this time she didn't. She continued to gaze at him with big, bright eyes full of trust. Her words hung in the air, and he knew it was far too late to pretend he didn't want this moment to go on endlessly.

"That's a promise, Miss Henner," he said.

Her lips tipped up in a sweet little half smile. He wondered if he was grinning like a fool as he leaned toward her, only to realize at the same time she was leaning toward him. His fingers tangled in her thick chestnut hair as their lips met for a kiss.

He held her gently, careful not to ask anything of her. When her eyes met his once again, he hoped she could see all the assurances he could give her. Whatever they had been through, wherever the road might take them, he wanted to always be there for her.

He was trying to find the right words to tell her just that when they were both rattled by the booming sound of the first rocket sent up at the fairgrounds. It was merely an attention-getter; the concussion reverberated off the clock tower and the other buildings around them. The little puff of smoke visible against the deep azure of the night sky was already drifting on the breeze.

"I guess the big event is getting ready to start!" she exclaimed, reaching to pat Timber and reassure him.

Jake had to laugh as he agreed with her. "Yep, I'm pretty sure it is."

The air crackled with anticipation now, and probably nervous tension. Would she comment on their kiss? Was he supposed to ignore that it happened? What if he misread her and she felt only professional gratitude toward him after today? He was kind of glad there'd soon be a volley of noisy fireworks so he didn't have to think of something to say.

"Too bad they don't do the fireworks show farther out of town," he said awkwardly as they waited in silence. "They'd probably be spectacular out on the wide-open range, with the huge sky and no city lights in the way."

"Good idea," she replied. "I might suggest that to the committee next year. If I still have access to Juniper Ridge, that is."

"Of course, you will! It'll all be sorted by then."

"Maybe, but I did some checking this afternoon. Stackler really did drain my aunt and uncle dry, you know? Roy wasn't selling just because he was tired of ranching, but because he owes a bunch of back taxes, and there are liens from people he hasn't paid. He's nearly lost the place, and I don't think there's any way to avoid selling it now. It'll probably go for a fraction of what it's worth."

"I think that's what the new buyer is hoping."

She shot him a look. "You know who it is?"

"I probably shouldn't say anything…"

"Can you at least give me a hint?"

"I was sworn to secrecy!"

"It's not someone who wants to turn it into a housing development, is it? Not a golf course, I hope."

"No, nothing like that. I think you'll approve of the new buyer, as a matter of fact."

"Who is it already?" She laughed and shoved his shoulder playfully.

He was helpless to keep the truth from her any longer. "It's your boss, Judge Torres. He found out your uncle was having trouble, so he swooped in. He sent an agent to represent him. I don't even think Roy knew who this mysterious buyer was. But he's serious about it, Willie. He's not letting that place get away from you."

"He can't buy the ranch for me! That's crazy! What is he thinking?"

"Hey, don't scold me about it, you've got to take it up with him. All I know is what he told me. He and Elisa want to do this for you. You belong on Juniper Ridge, Willie. It's what your grandfather wanted—he got cheated as much as you did. Besides, the judge loves you like you're his own daughter."

"But it's too much!"

Jake had to laugh at her continued protests. "So you're going to tell the richest man in the county he can't do something nice for you? Boy, you sure like to make things hard on yourself."

"I don't like to rely on people. It's usually better if I just—"

"If you just what?" Jake said, cocking one eyebrow in mock accusation.

She must've realized what she'd been about to say. After their conversation only minutes ago, he felt it was his duty to remind her that learning to rely on others might not be such a bad thing. She gave a self-deprecating chuckle and shook her head before continuing.

"If I just remember that I'm not in charge of everything. Is that better?"

"Much better. I think you've made some real progress there, Willie, and—"

His words were cut off by a series of loud bangs overhead. The display was starting in earnest now. He leaned back into the cushions to take in the show. Willie was close so he slipped his arm around her shoulders.

A quick volley of rockets whizzed up into the sky, exploding in glorious color and sound. They sizzled as the remnants fanned out, filling the visible area overhead and taking away any words between them. As Willie had promised, the bold edifice of the courthouse made an impressive set piece against the blazing display.

"Wow," Willie said, her breath coming out as a peaceful sigh.

She rested against him as Timber settled at their feet. They watched the next brilliant wave of fireworks fill the world with dazzling light, dancing high above them. Jake couldn't ever remember fireworks being so beautiful.

"Yeah," he agreed. "Wow."

# Epilogue

Willie found a quiet corner to catch her breath. The familiar landscape around her was a vibrant palette of springtime colors. Rolling hills glowed with the bright green of new grasses against the sun-bleached pale of the rocky earth, while swaths of bluebonnets, buttercups and fiery gaillardia painted a masterpiece no human hand could ever recreate. The breeze carried the scents of mountain laurel and a smoky barbecue, along with the sounds of children playing.

She could see them from where she stood at the side of the house. Shaye was running down the hillside with some friends, laughing as they went. Timber trotted along after them. Any moment now their mothers would start calling them back, reminding them not to ruin their good clothes. Willie was glad she'd asked everyone to bring something casual to change into today after the ceremony.

And what a beautiful ceremony it had been! Willie had told everyone she didn't want too much fuss, but, of course, they had all fussed. The flowers were abundant, the music was inspired and Willie's gown was a fairy-tale dream come true. When she had walked down that aisle in the same church where she'd been baptized, it had never looked so special to her. A big part of that was the man who waited for her at the altar.

He came up beside her now, startling her from her musings.

"So here you are, hiding behind the house," Jake said, wrapping his arms around her, pressing his lips to her cheek. "Everything okay?"

"Everything is perfect," she said. "Thank you for encouraging me to have the reception here at Juniper Ridge. There's room for the kids to play, plenty of parking and the food tent looks really nice set up by the old horse paddock."

"We've got the best barbecue in Texas here today, and all the biscuits and pie you can possibly want from Mama May's."

"I can't wait. I wanted to get a couple minutes to gather myself before we head back there to everyone. I can't believe so many people came out today!"

"It was your brilliant idea to invite the whole church and half the county."

"That was a brilliant idea, wasn't it? Well, they voted for you, Sheriff, so I guess the least we can do is invite them to the wedding. But wow…for the first time ever, I feel like I have a large family."

She loved the sound of his laughter when he chuckled at her words. "You *do* have a large family. Look around, Willie. You've got my parents now, all my aunts and uncles and cousins, and there's Jess and Shaye. And, of course, Abby and Mac and Maggie, plus her parents. There's Judge Torres and Elisa…and Garret! Who could ever have guessed he'd be part of your family again?"

Now it was Willie's turn to laugh. "I never would have, but he's been great. He's a huge help, trying to get the ranch running properly again."

"It looks like Abby and Mac are glad to have him around, too."

"He's really come through for them," she said.

"And he helped get your aunt's studio all cleaned out. Are you still planning to have Jess and her students come to paint that mural you talked about?"

"Absolutely! The whole back wall, all done in bright colors, with the kids painting portraits of people they love."

"I think that's a wonderful tribute to your mother. She'd be so proud of you, Willie."

"She died there in that studio, Jake. I have to do *something* to put life and joy back into the space."

"Your plan is perfect. Jess is flattered you asked for her help with it."

"I couldn't do it without her! It's just…sometimes it all feels like too much. It's so much more than I ever dared hope for."

"But isn't that what grace is all about? I love you, Willie. I'm blessed beyond belief that you have chosen to become my wife. I'm going to do everything I possibly can to deserve you. You know as well as I do that good times don't always last, but I trust God to get us through whatever comes along. I'm looking forward to a lifetime of grace with you, Willie, the good times *and* the bad."

She turned to face him, looping her arms around his neck. "I love you so much, Sheriff Richards. Thank you for always reminding me what's really important. Oh, and thanks for arranging the caterer. I'm so glad I let everyone help me with all this! The food smells amazing."

"It does, doesn't it? We'd better head out there and get this party started."

"We will...eventually," she said. "For now, I think I'd like to keep you all to myself for a little while longer."

He gave her a grin that made her weak in the knees as he spoke those three words every woman longed to hear.

"Well, yes, ma'am."

\* \* \* \* \*

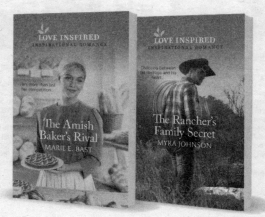

# Get 4 FREE REWARDS!

**We'll send you 2 FREE Books <u>plus</u> 2 FREE Mystery Gifts.**

**FREE**
Value Over
**$20**

Both the **Love Inspired®** and **Love Inspired®** Suspense series feature compelling novels filled with inspirational romance, faith, forgiveness, and hope.

---

**YES!** Please send me 2 FREE novels from the Love Inspired or Love Inspired Suspense series and my 2 FREE gifts (gifts are worth about $10 retail). After receiving them, if I don't wish to receive any more books, I can return the shipping statement marked "cancel." If I don't cancel, I will receive 6 brand-new Love Inspired Larger-Print books or Love Inspired Suspense Larger-Print books every month and be billed just $6.24 each in the U.S. or $6.49 each in Canada. That is a savings of at least 17% off the cover price. It's quite a bargain! Shipping and handling is just 50¢ per book in the U.S. and $1.25 per book in Canada.* I understand that accepting the 2 free books and gifts places me under no obligation to buy anything. I can always return a shipment and cancel at any time by calling the number below. The free books and gifts are mine to keep no matter what I decide.

Choose one: ☐ **Love Inspired**
**Larger-Print**
(122/322 IDN GRDF)

☐ **Love Inspired Suspense**
**Larger-Print**
(107/307 IDN GRDF)

Name (please print)

Address                                                                                          Apt. #

City                                          State/Province                          Zip/Postal Code

**Email:** Please check this box ☐ if you would like to receive newsletters and promotional emails from Harlequin Enterprises ULC and its affiliates. You can unsubscribe anytime.

### Mail to the **Harlequin Reader Service:**
**IN U.S.A.:** P.O. Box 1341, Buffalo, NY 14240-8531
**IN CANADA:** P.O. Box 603, Fort Erie, Ontario L2A 5X3

**Want to try 2 free books from another series! Call 1-800-873-8635 or visit www.ReaderService.com.**

---

LIRLIS22R2

# HARLEQUIN
## PLUS

Announcing a **BRAND-NEW** multimedia subscription service for romance fans like you!

---

## Read, Watch and Play.

Experience the easiest way to get the romance content you crave.

Start your **FREE 7 DAY TRIAL** at
<u>www.harlequinplus.com/freetrial</u>.

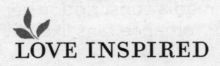

"Oh, no," Mike whispered. "Not here, too."

A heavy stone of foreboding dropped in Julia's stomach as she slowly rose and pivoted to look at whatever Mike had just seen.

A fire was beginning to curl up the side of the cabin next door. It was maybe thirty yards away, separated by a dozen trees—and a pile of chopped wood that stretched between the cabins like one long dynamite fuse.

How could this have happened? There'd been no lightning. No one was staying in the other cabins. There was no reason a fire could spontaneously begin next door. There was only one answer—

The evil that had been setting Crooked Valley on fire had followed them here. Why?

"Daddy! There's a fire!" Ginny pointed at the orange flames eagerly running up the wooden siding of the cabin next door, inches away from the woodpile. Any hope Julia had that her eyes were deceiving her disappeared. The house next door was on fire, and their lives were suddenly in very real danger.

"We need to get out of here. Now." Mike grabbed Ginny's coat and started helping her arms into the sleeves. Julia bent down beside him and fastened the zipper, then grabbed Ginny's hat and tugged it on her head as Mike pulled back on his boots. Julia grabbed her coat just in time to see the flames leap to the pile of dried wood and race across the top like a hungry animal.

Heading straight for their cabin.

"Get in my car!" Mike shouted.

They ran for the SUV, but Julia stopped short just as Mike opened the passenger-side door. "Mike, look." The two front tires had been slashed. Julia spun to the right and saw the same thing had been done to her car. "Someone doesn't want us leaving," she said under her breath. Fear curled a tight fist inside her chest.

Mike quickly scanned the area. "He's out there. Somewhere."

Oh, God. Why would the arsonist follow them? Why would he target Mike and Ginny? Or Julia, for that matter?

A chill snaked up her spine as she realized the arsonist must have *watched* them stringing lights, singing Christmas carols. He'd watched them—and still decided to take the lives of two adults and a small child. What kind of evil person did that?

"Come on. We have to go on foot." Mike took Julia's hand in one hand, then scooped up Ginny with the other.

Even as he said the words, she could see the fire overtaking the small cabin, eagerly devouring the Christmas lights they had just hung. The sweet moment the three of them had was being erased.

It was a two-mile trip down the mountain. Another two miles back to town. On foot, they'd never make it before dark. How were they going to get back to safety?

*Don't miss*
Refuge Up in Flames *by Shirley Jump,*
*available December 2022 wherever*
*Love Inspired books and ebooks are sold.*

LoveInspired.com